Walt Disney's Donald Duck

A Fluid Situation

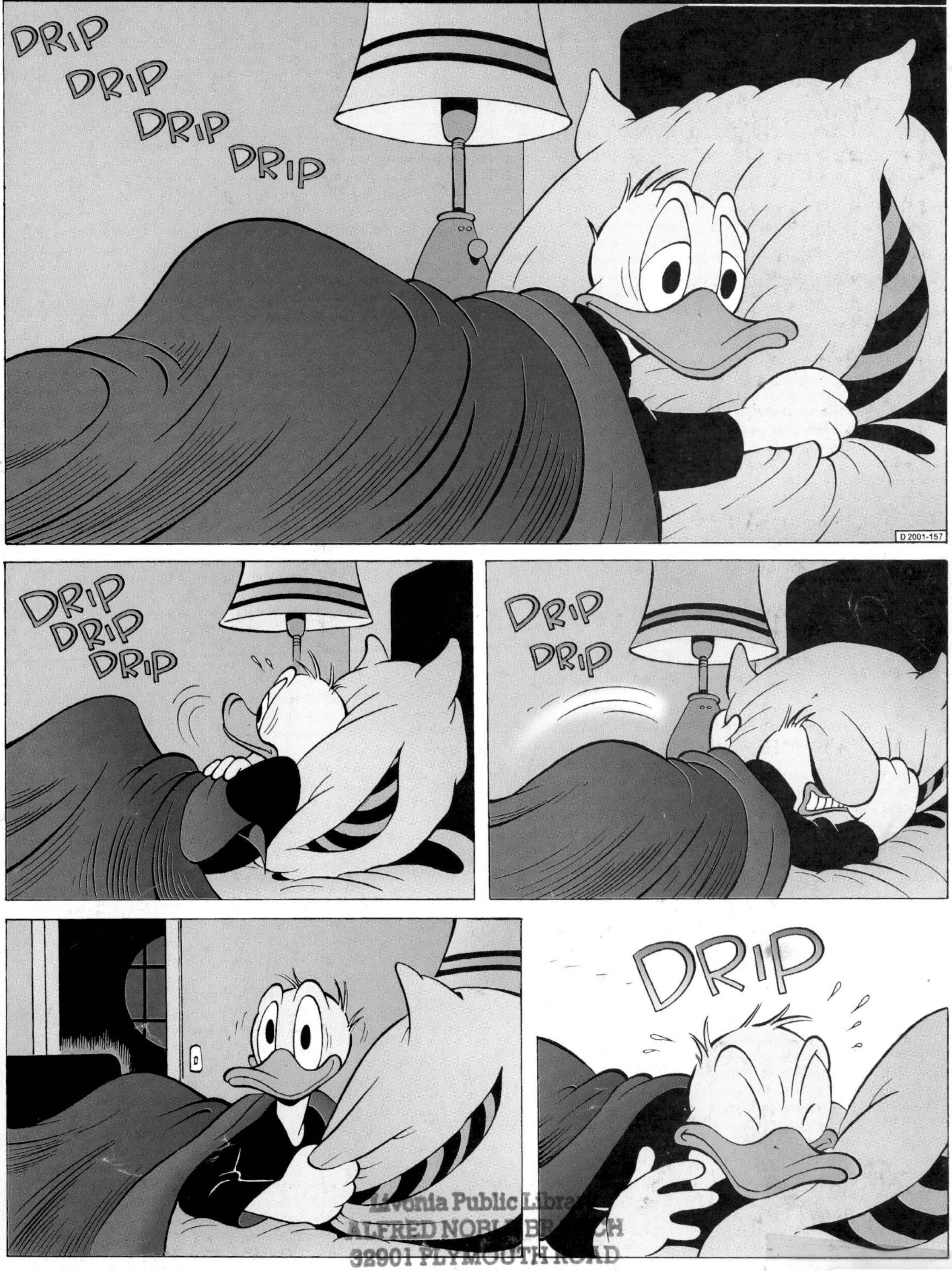
DRIP
DRIP
DRIP
DRIP
D 2001-157
DRIP
DRIP
DRIP
DRIP
DRIP
DRIP

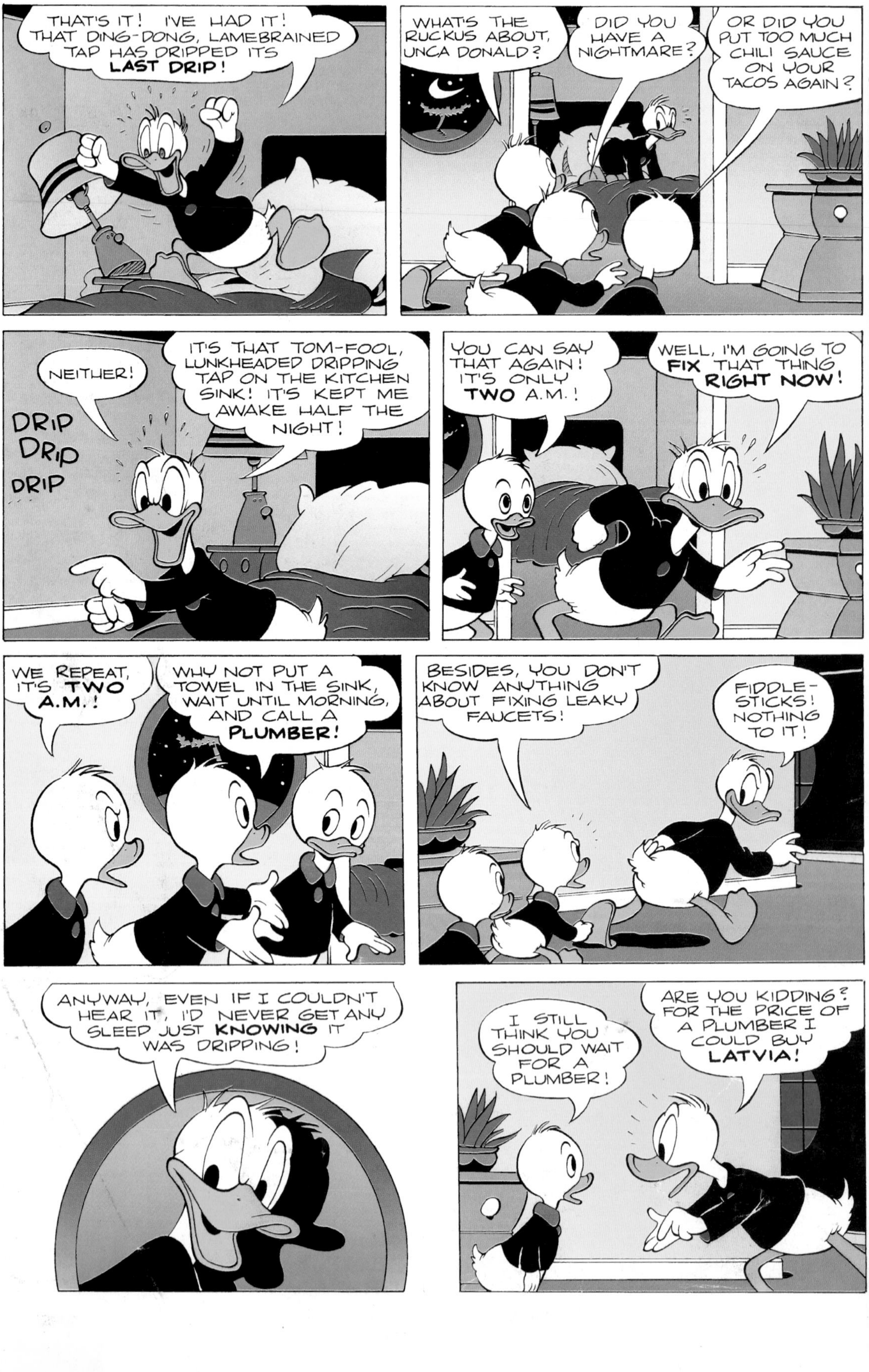
THAT'S IT! I'VE HAD IT! THAT DING-DONG, LAMEBRAINED TAP HAS DRIPPED ITS **LAST DRIP**!
WHAT'S THE RUCKUS ABOUT, UNCA DONALD?
DID YOU HAVE A NIGHTMARE?
OR DID YOU PUT TOO MUCH CHILI SAUCE ON YOUR TACOS AGAIN?
NEITHER!
IT'S THAT TOM-FOOL, LUNKHEADED DRIPPING TAP ON THE KITCHEN SINK! IT'S KEPT ME AWAKE HALF THE NIGHT!
DRIP DRIP DRIP
YOU CAN SAY THAT AGAIN! IT'S ONLY **TWO** A.M.!
WELL, I'M GOING TO **FIX** THAT THING **RIGHT NOW**!
WE REPEAT, IT'S **TWO A.M.**!
WHY NOT PUT A TOWEL IN THE SINK, WAIT UNTIL MORNING, AND CALL A **PLUMBER**!
BESIDES, YOU DON'T KNOW ANYTHING ABOUT FIXING LEAKY FAUCETS!
FIDDLE-STICKS! NOTHING TO IT!
ANYWAY, EVEN IF I COULDN'T HEAR IT, I'D NEVER GET ANY SLEEP JUST **KNOWING** IT WAS DRIPPING!
I STILL THINK YOU SHOULD WAIT FOR A PLUMBER!
ARE YOU KIDDING? FOR THE PRICE OF A PLUMBER I COULD BUY **LATVIA**!

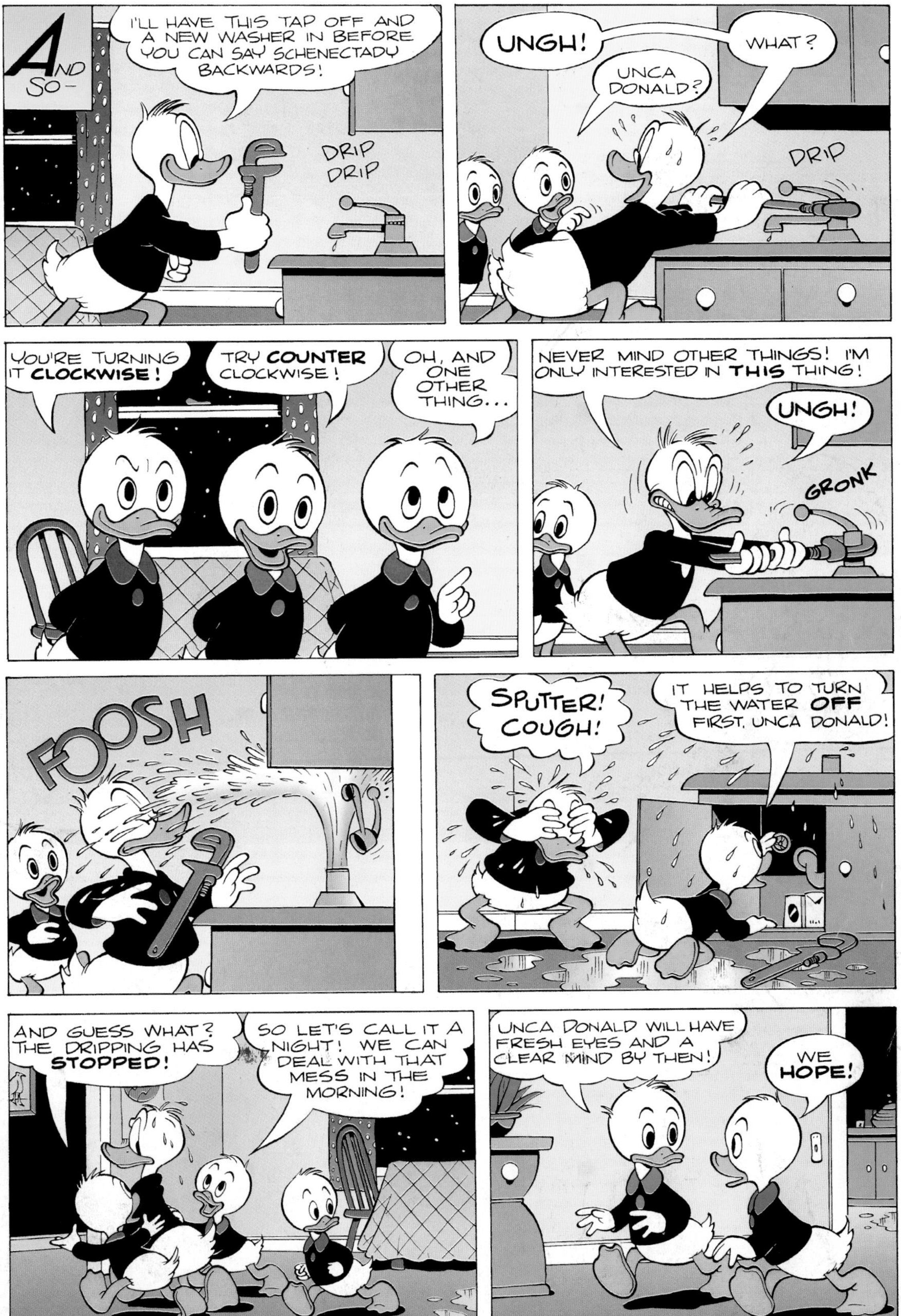
AND SO–
I'LL HAVE THIS TAP OFF AND A NEW WASHER IN BEFORE YOU CAN SAY SCHENECTADY BACKWARDS!
DRIP DRIP
UNGH!
WHAT?
UNCA DONALD?
DRIP
YOU'RE TURNING IT **CLOCKWISE**!
TRY **COUNTER** CLOCKWISE!
OH, AND ONE OTHER THING...
NEVER MIND OTHER THINGS! I'M ONLY INTERESTED IN **THIS** THING!
UNGH!
GRONK
FOOSH
SPUTTER! COUGH!
IT HELPS TO TURN THE WATER **OFF** FIRST, UNCA DONALD!
AND GUESS WHAT? THE DRIPPING HAS **STOPPED**!
SO LET'S CALL IT A NIGHT! WE CAN DEAL WITH THAT MESS IN THE MORNING!
UNCA DONALD WILL HAVE FRESH EYES AND A CLEAR MIND BY THEN!
WE **HOPE**!

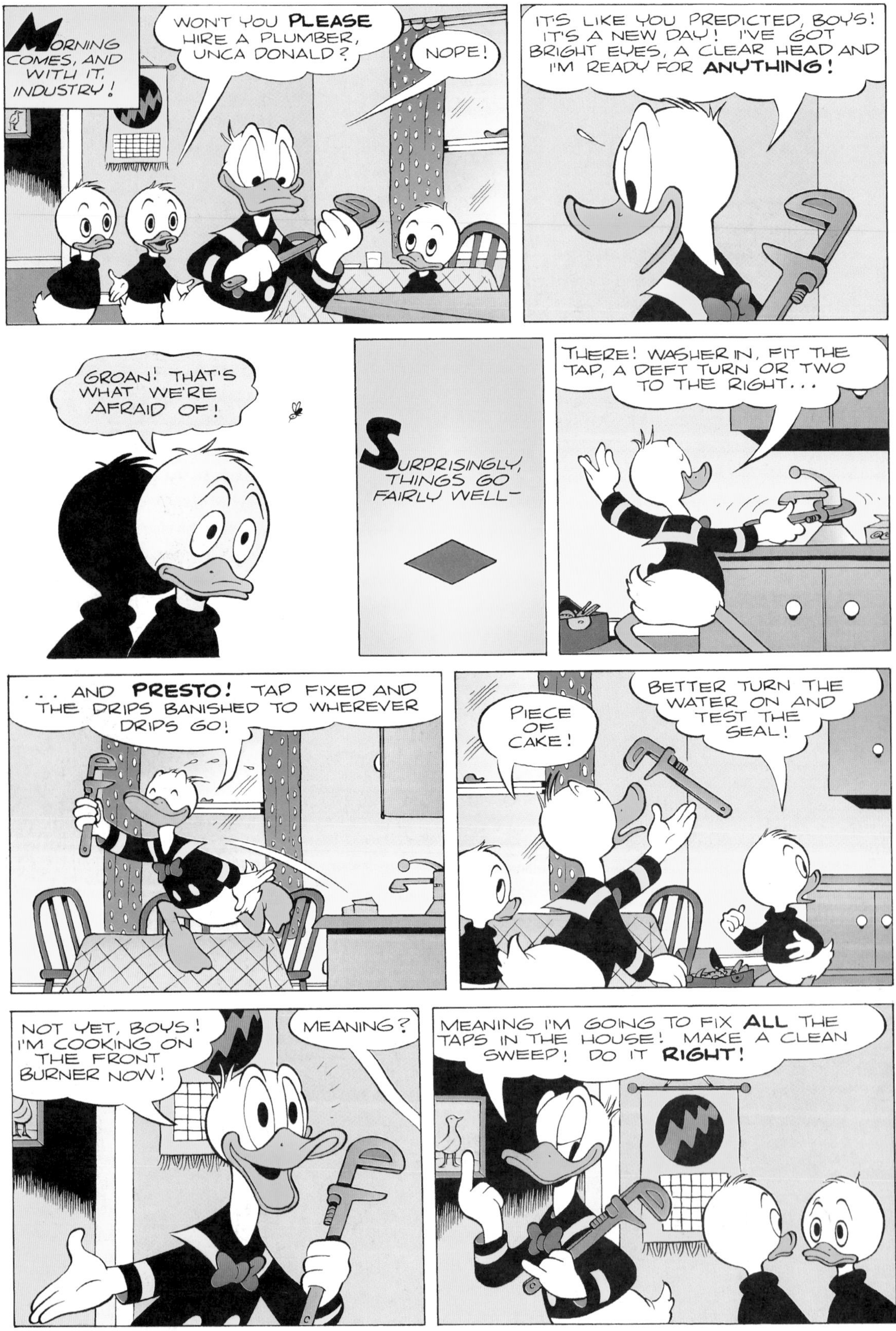
MORNING COMES, AND WITH IT, INDUSTRY!
WON'T YOU PLEASE HIRE A PLUMBER, UNCA DONALD?
NOPE!
IT'S LIKE YOU PREDICTED, BOYS! IT'S A NEW DAY! I'VE GOT BRIGHT EYES, A CLEAR HEAD AND I'M READY FOR ANYTHING!
GROAN! THAT'S WHAT WE'RE AFRAID OF!
SURPRISINGLY, THINGS GO FAIRLY WELL—
THERE! WASHER IN, FIT THE TAP, A DEFT TURN OR TWO TO THE RIGHT...
... AND PRESTO! TAP FIXED AND THE DRIPS BANISHED TO WHEREVER DRIPS GO!
PIECE OF CAKE!
BETTER TURN THE WATER ON AND TEST THE SEAL!
NOT YET, BOYS! I'M COOKING ON THE FRONT BURNER NOW!
MEANING?
MEANING I'M GOING TO FIX ALL THE TAPS IN THE HOUSE! MAKE A CLEAN SWEEP! DO IT RIGHT!

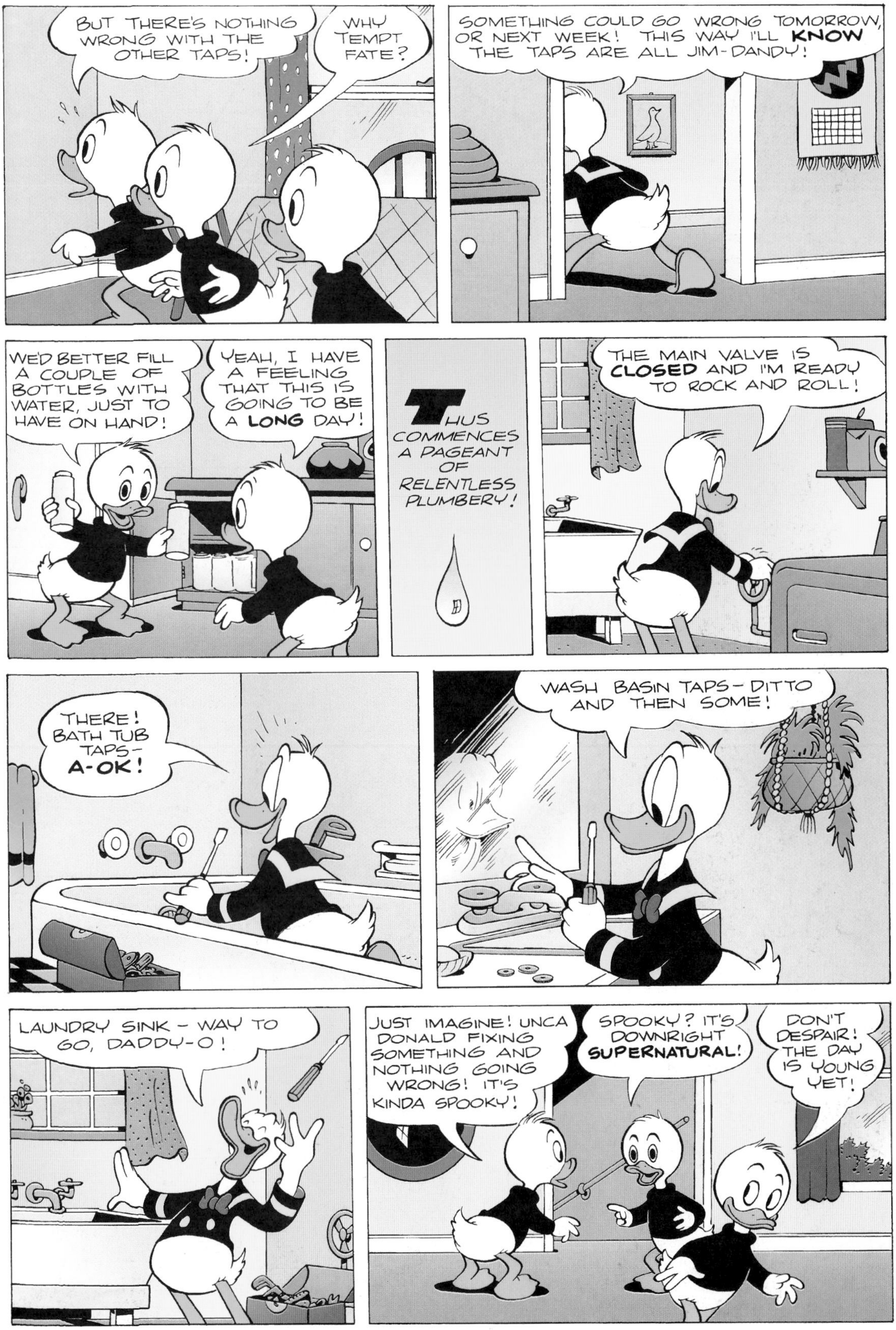
BUT THERE'S NOTHING WRONG WITH THE OTHER TAPS!
WHY TEMPT FATE?
SOMETHING COULD GO WRONG TOMORROW, OR NEXT WEEK! THIS WAY I'LL KNOW THE TAPS ARE ALL JIM-DANDY!
WE'D BETTER FILL A COUPLE OF BOTTLES WITH WATER, JUST TO HAVE ON HAND!
YEAH, I HAVE A FEELING THAT THIS IS GOING TO BE A LONG DAY!
THUS COMMENCES A PAGEANT OF RELENTLESS PLUMBERY!
THE MAIN VALVE IS CLOSED AND I'M READY TO ROCK AND ROLL!
THERE! BATH TUB TAPS— A-OK!
WASH BASIN TAPS— DITTO AND THEN SOME!
LAUNDRY SINK — WAY TO GO, DADDY-O!
JUST IMAGINE! UNCA DONALD FIXING SOMETHING AND NOTHING GOING WRONG! IT'S KINDA SPOOKY!
SPOOKY? IT'S DOWNRIGHT SUPERNATURAL!
DON'T DESPAIR! THE DAY IS YOUNG YET!

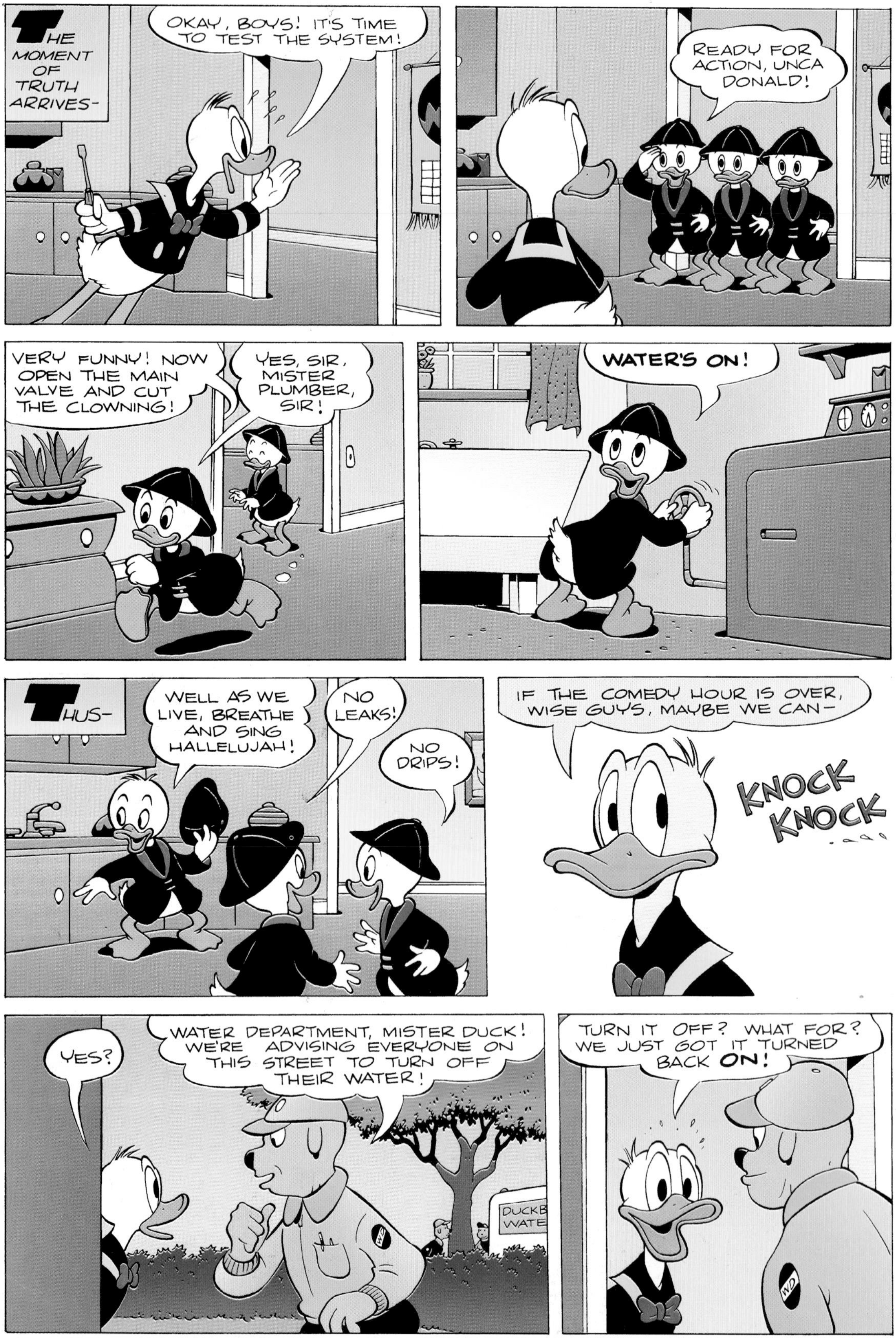
THE MOMENT OF TRUTH ARRIVES-
OKAY, BOYS! IT'S TIME TO TEST THE SYSTEM!
READY FOR ACTION, UNCA DONALD!
VERY FUNNY! NOW OPEN THE MAIN VALVE AND CUT THE CLOWNING!
YES, SIR, MISTER PLUMBER, SIR!
WATER'S ON!
THUS-
WELL AS WE LIVE, BREATHE AND SING HALLELUJAH!
NO LEAKS!
NO DRIPS!
IF THE COMEDY HOUR IS OVER, WISE GUYS, MAYBE WE CAN-
KNOCK KNOCK
YES?
WATER DEPARTMENT, MISTER DUCK! WE'RE ADVISING EVERYONE ON THIS STREET TO TURN OFF THEIR WATER!
TURN IT OFF? WHAT FOR? WE JUST GOT IT TURNED BACK ON!

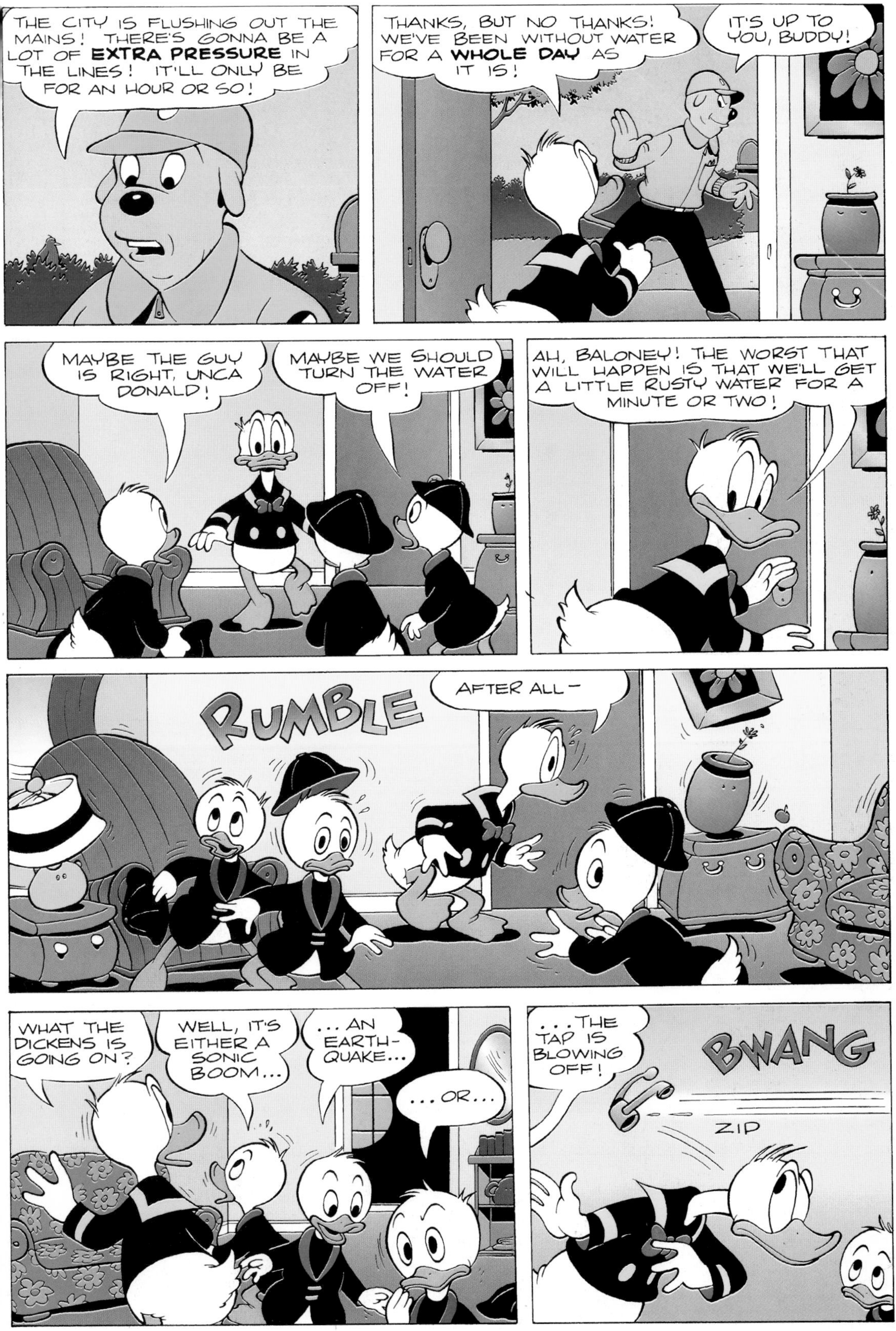
THE CITY IS FLUSHING OUT THE MAINS! THERE'S GONNA BE A LOT OF **EXTRA PRESSURE** IN THE LINES! IT'LL ONLY BE FOR AN HOUR OR SO!
THANKS, BUT NO THANKS! WE'VE BEEN WITHOUT WATER FOR A **WHOLE DAY** AS IT IS!
IT'S UP TO YOU, BUDDY!
MAYBE THE GUY IS RIGHT, UNCA DONALD!
MAYBE WE SHOULD TURN THE WATER OFF!
AH, BALONEY! THE WORST THAT WILL HAPPEN IS THAT WE'LL GET A LITTLE RUSTY WATER FOR A MINUTE OR TWO!
RUMBLE
AFTER ALL–
WHAT THE DICKENS IS GOING ON?
WELL, IT'S EITHER A SONIC BOOM...
... AN EARTH-QUAKE...
... OR ...
... THE TAP IS BLOWING OFF!
BWANG
ZIP

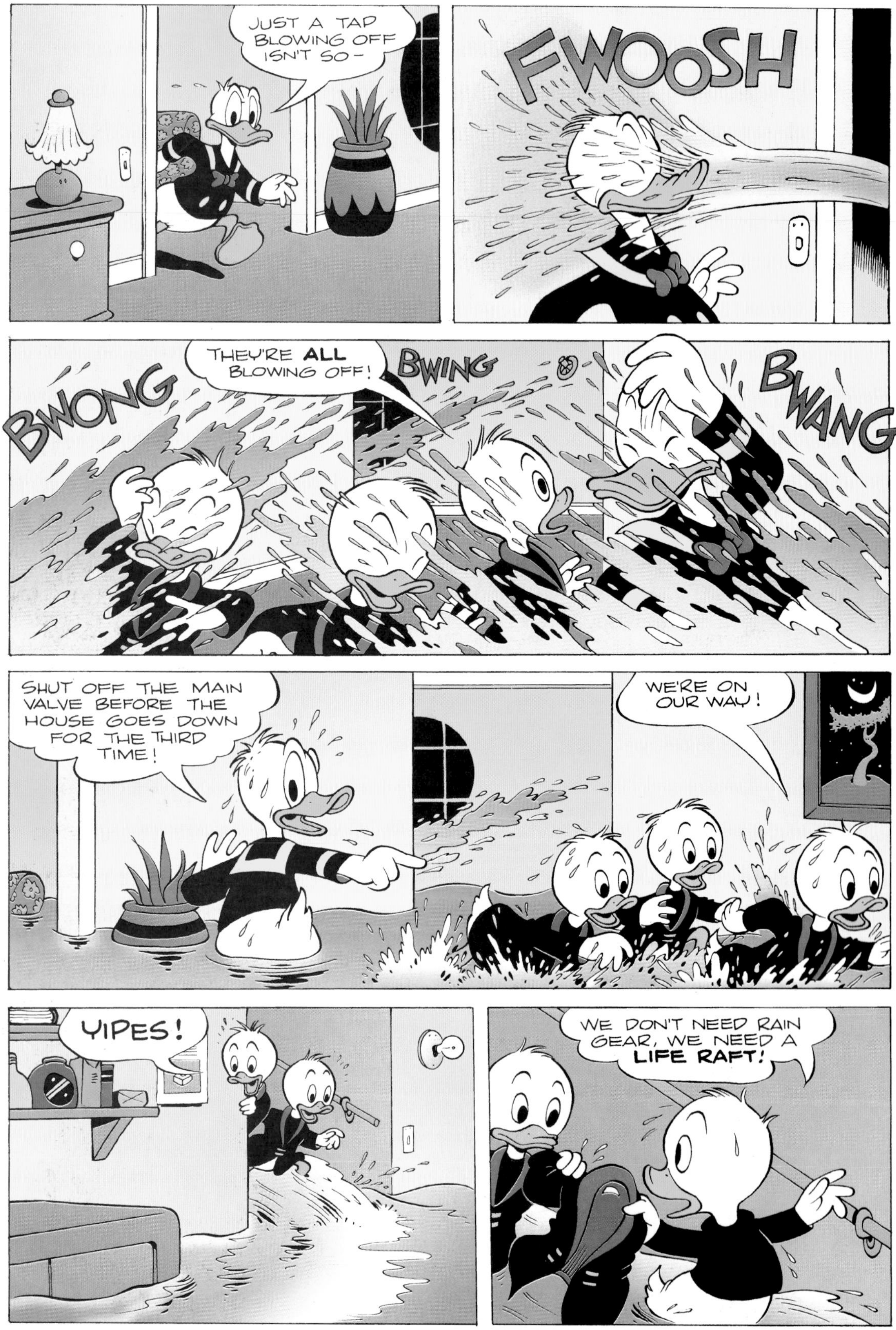

JUST A TAP BLOWING OFF ISN'T SO–
FWOOSH
BWONG
THEY'RE ALL BLOWING OFF!
BWING
BWANG
SHUT OFF THE MAIN VALVE BEFORE THE HOUSE GOES DOWN FOR THE THIRD TIME!
WE'RE ON OUR WAY!
YIPES!
WE DON'T NEED RAIN GEAR, WE NEED A LIFE RAFT!

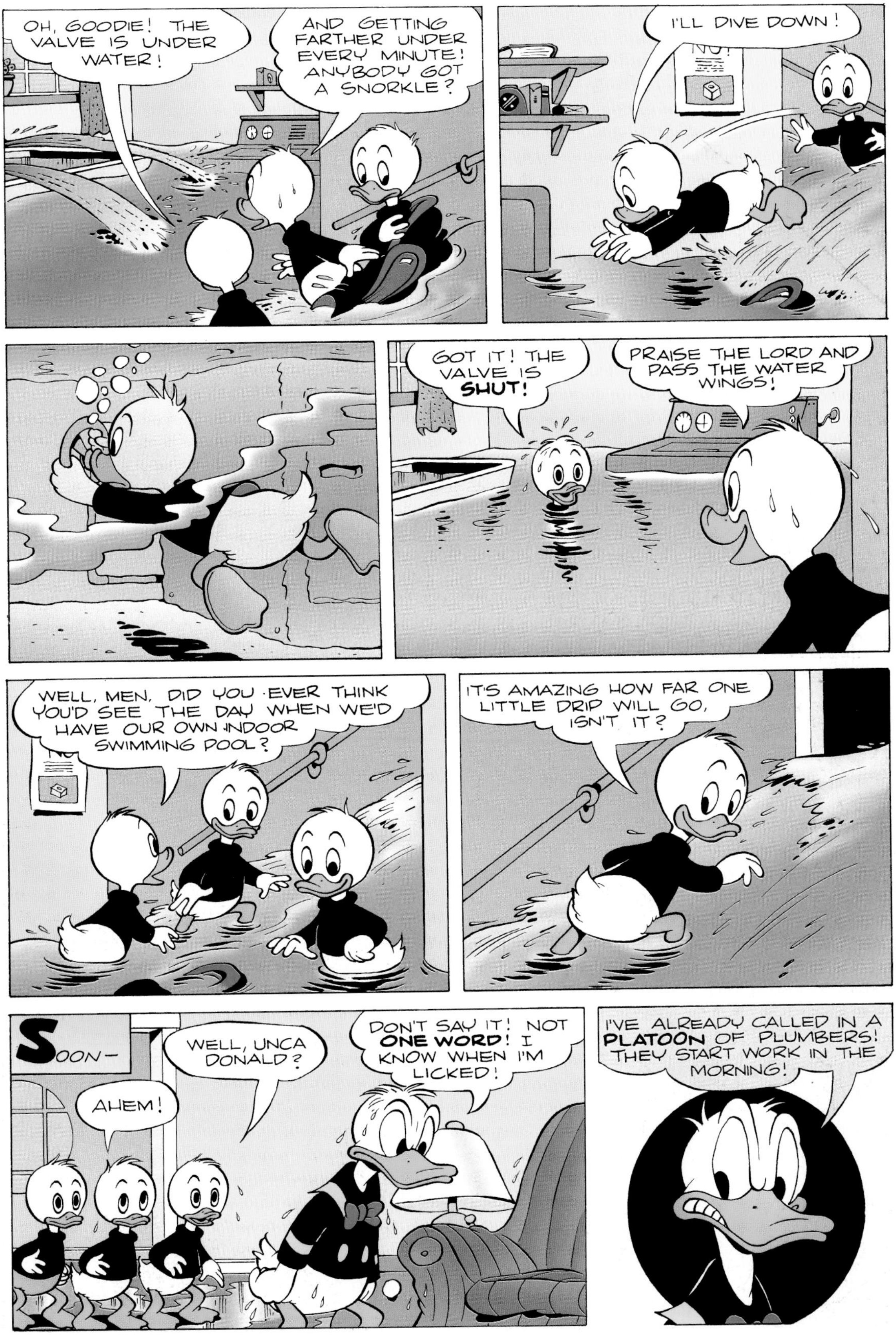
OH, GOODIE! THE VALVE IS UNDER WATER!
AND GETTING FARTHER UNDER EVERY MINUTE! ANYBODY GOT A SNORKLE?
I'LL DIVE DOWN!
GOT IT! THE VALVE IS SHUT!
PRAISE THE LORD AND PASS THE WATER WINGS!
WELL, MEN, DID YOU EVER THINK YOU'D SEE THE DAY WHEN WE'D HAVE OUR OWN INDOOR SWIMMING POOL?
IT'S AMAZING HOW FAR ONE LITTLE DRIP WILL GO, ISN'T IT?
SOON—
AHEM!
WELL, UNCA DONALD?
DON'T SAY IT! NOT ONE WORD! I KNOW WHEN I'M LICKED!
I'VE ALREADY CALLED IN A PLATOON OF PLUMBERS! THEY START WORK IN THE MORNING!

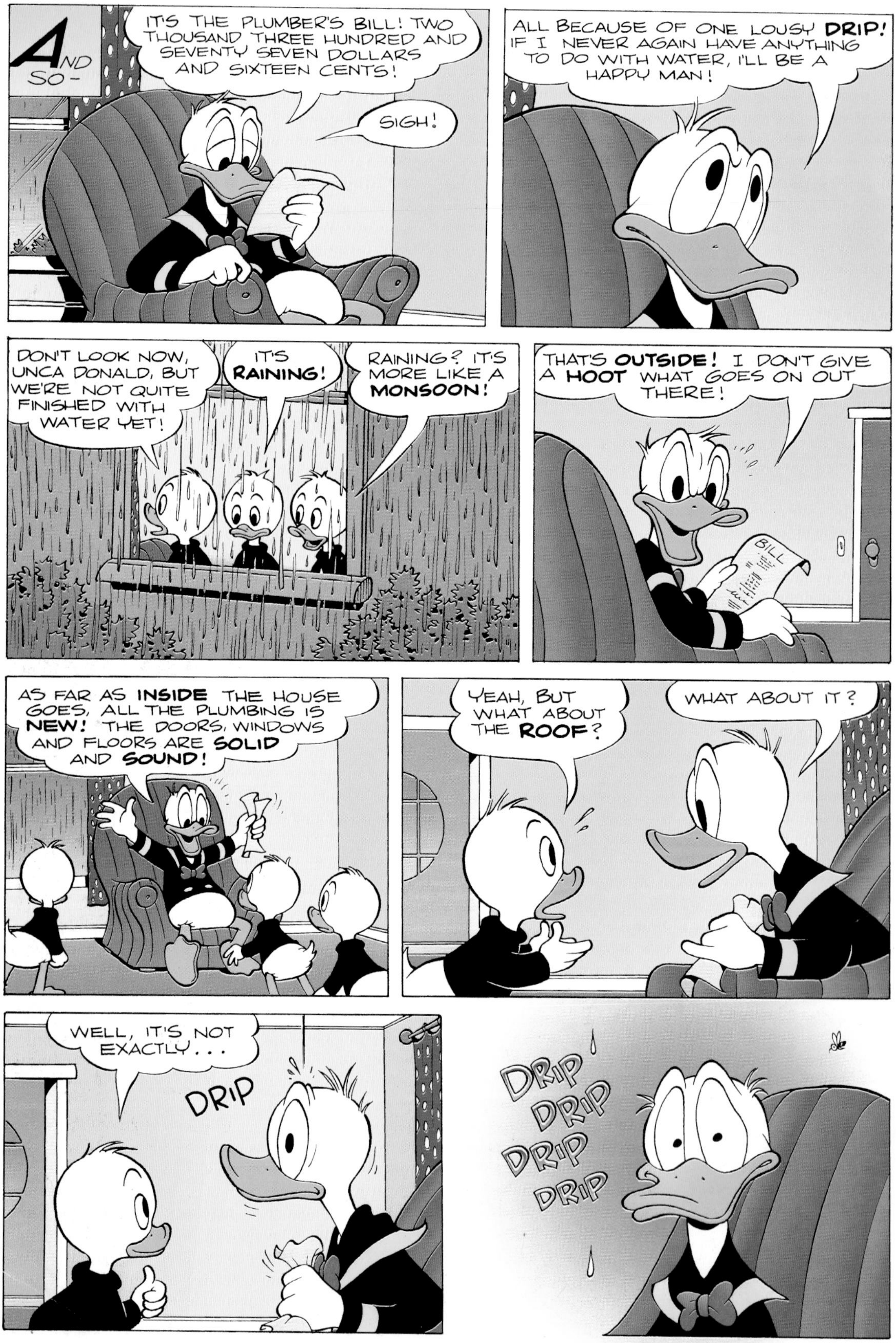
AND SO-
IT'S THE PLUMBER'S BILL! TWO THOUSAND THREE HUNDRED AND SEVENTY SEVEN DOLLARS AND SIXTEEN CENTS!
SIGH!
ALL BECAUSE OF ONE LOUSY DRIP! IF I NEVER AGAIN HAVE ANYTHING TO DO WITH WATER, I'LL BE A HAPPY MAN!
DON'T LOOK NOW, UNCA DONALD, BUT WE'RE NOT QUITE FINISHED WITH WATER YET!
IT'S RAINING!
RAINING? IT'S MORE LIKE A MONSOON!
THAT'S OUTSIDE! I DON'T GIVE A HOOT WHAT GOES ON OUT THERE!
BILL
AS FAR AS INSIDE THE HOUSE GOES, ALL THE PLUMBING IS NEW! THE DOORS, WINDOWS AND FLOORS ARE SOLID AND SOUND!
YEAH, BUT WHAT ABOUT THE ROOF?
WHAT ABOUT IT?
WELL, IT'S NOT EXACTLY...
DRIP
DRIP DRIP DRIP DRIP

Walt Disney's Mickey Mouse in Easy Work

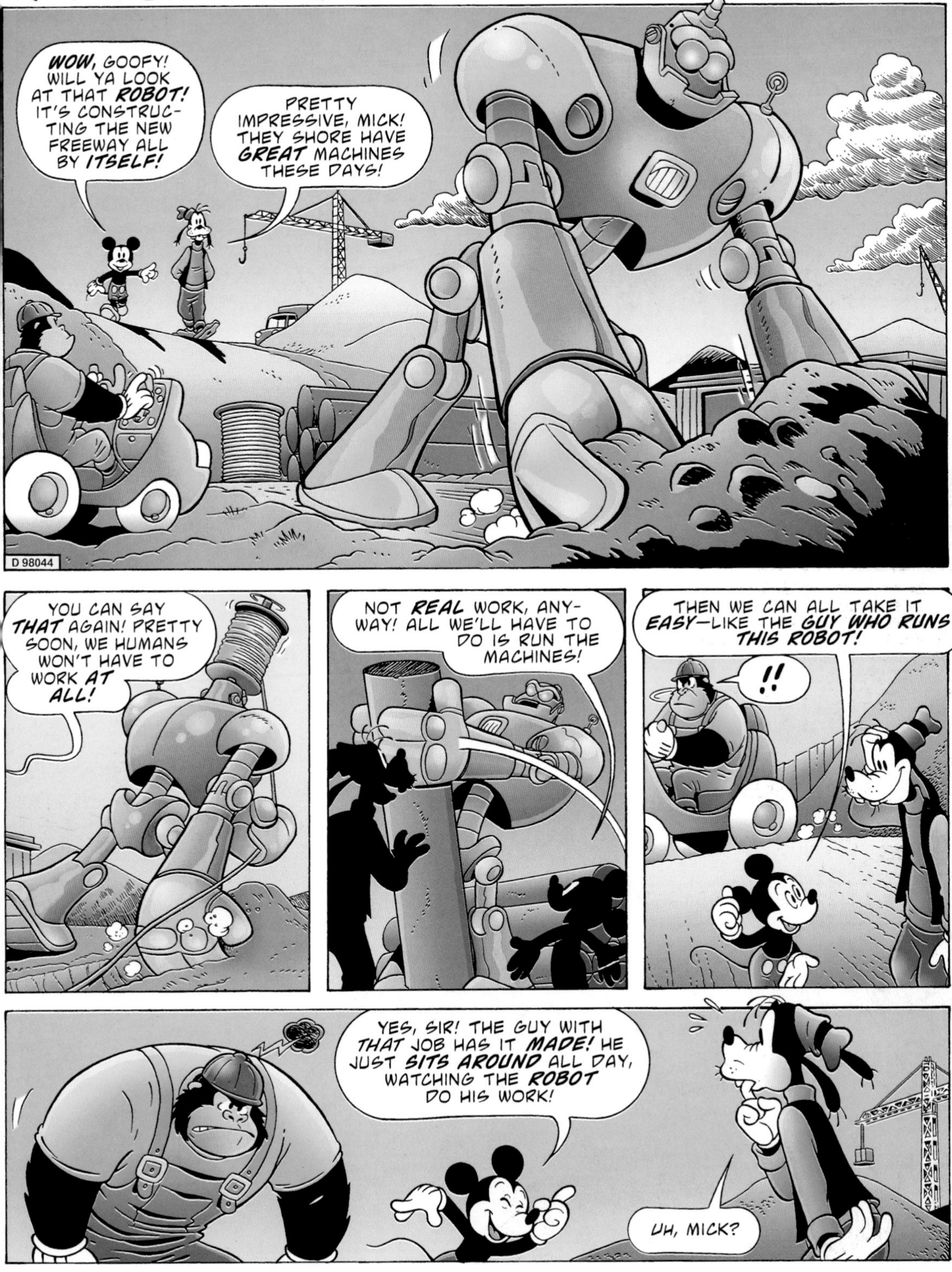

WOW, GOOFY! WILL YA LOOK AT THAT ROBOT! IT'S CONSTRUCTING THE NEW FREEWAY ALL BY ITSELF!
PRETTY IMPRESSIVE, MICK! THEY SHORE HAVE GREAT MACHINES THESE DAYS!
D 98044
YOU CAN SAY THAT AGAIN! PRETTY SOON, WE HUMANS WON'T HAVE TO WORK AT ALL!
NOT REAL WORK, ANYWAY! ALL WE'LL HAVE TO DO IS RUN THE MACHINES!
THEN WE CAN ALL TAKE IT EASY—LIKE THE GUY WHO RUNS THIS ROBOT!
!!
YES, SIR! THE GUY WITH THAT JOB HAS IT MADE! HE JUST SITS AROUND ALL DAY, WATCHING THE ROBOT DO HIS WORK!
UH, MICK?

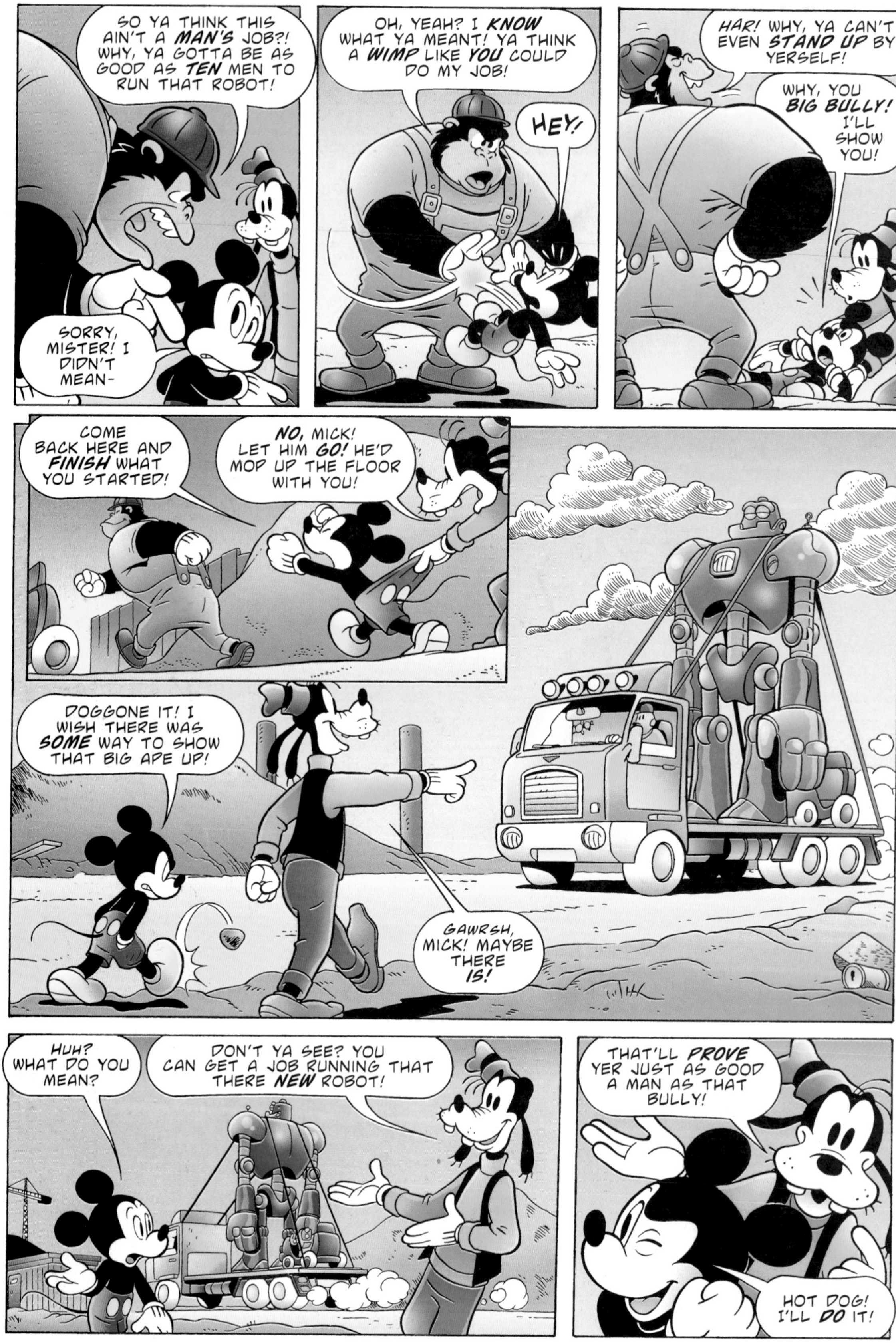
SO YA THINK THIS AIN'T A MAN'S JOB?! WHY, YA GOTTA BE AS GOOD AS TEN MEN TO RUN THAT ROBOT!
SORRY, MISTER! I DIDN'T MEAN-
OH, YEAH? I KNOW WHAT YA MEANT! YA THINK A WIMP LIKE YOU COULD DO MY JOB!
HEY!
HAR! WHY, YA CAN'T EVEN STAND UP BY YERSELF!
WHY, YOU BIG BULLY! I'LL SHOW YOU!
COME BACK HERE AND FINISH WHAT YOU STARTED!
NO, MICK! LET HIM GO! HE'D MOP UP THE FLOOR WITH YOU!
DOGGONE IT! I WISH THERE WAS SOME WAY TO SHOW THAT BIG APE UP!
GAWRSH, MICK! MAYBE THERE IS!
HUH? WHAT DO YOU MEAN?
DON'T YA SEE? YOU CAN GET A JOB RUNNING THAT THERE NEW ROBOT!
THAT'LL PROVE YER JUST AS GOOD A MAN AS THAT BULLY!
HOT DOG! I'LL DO IT!

GOOD LUCK, PAL!

THANKS, GOOFY! THIS MAY BE A BIG **MISTAKE**, BUT AT LEAST IT PROMISES TO BE **FUN**!

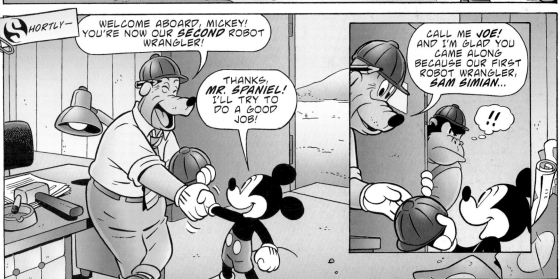

SHORTLY—

WELCOME ABOARD, MICKEY! YOU'RE NOW OUR **SECOND** ROBOT WRANGLER!

THANKS, **MR. SPANIEL!** I'LL TRY TO DO A GOOD JOB!

CALL ME **JOE!** AND I'M GLAD YOU CAME ALONG BECAUSE OUR FIRST ROBOT WRANGLER, **SAM SIMIAN**...

!!

...IS GETTING **TOO BIG FOR HIS BRITCHES!** THINKS HE'S THE **ONLY** ONE WHO CAN HANDLE ONE OF THESE GALOOTS!

GRRR!

BUT I THINK A **SMART** YOUNG FELLA LIKE YOU CAN PICK IT RIGHT UP, AND **STOP** HIS BRAGGING!

COUNT ON IT, JOE!

WELL, HERE WE—**SAM!** WHAT'RE **YOU** DOING HERE?

HIYA, JOE! JUST **CHECKING OUT** THE NEW EQUIPMENT! YES SIR, ANOTHER GOOD ONE!

SAY, WHO'S THE **LITTLE** GUY?

HMM...

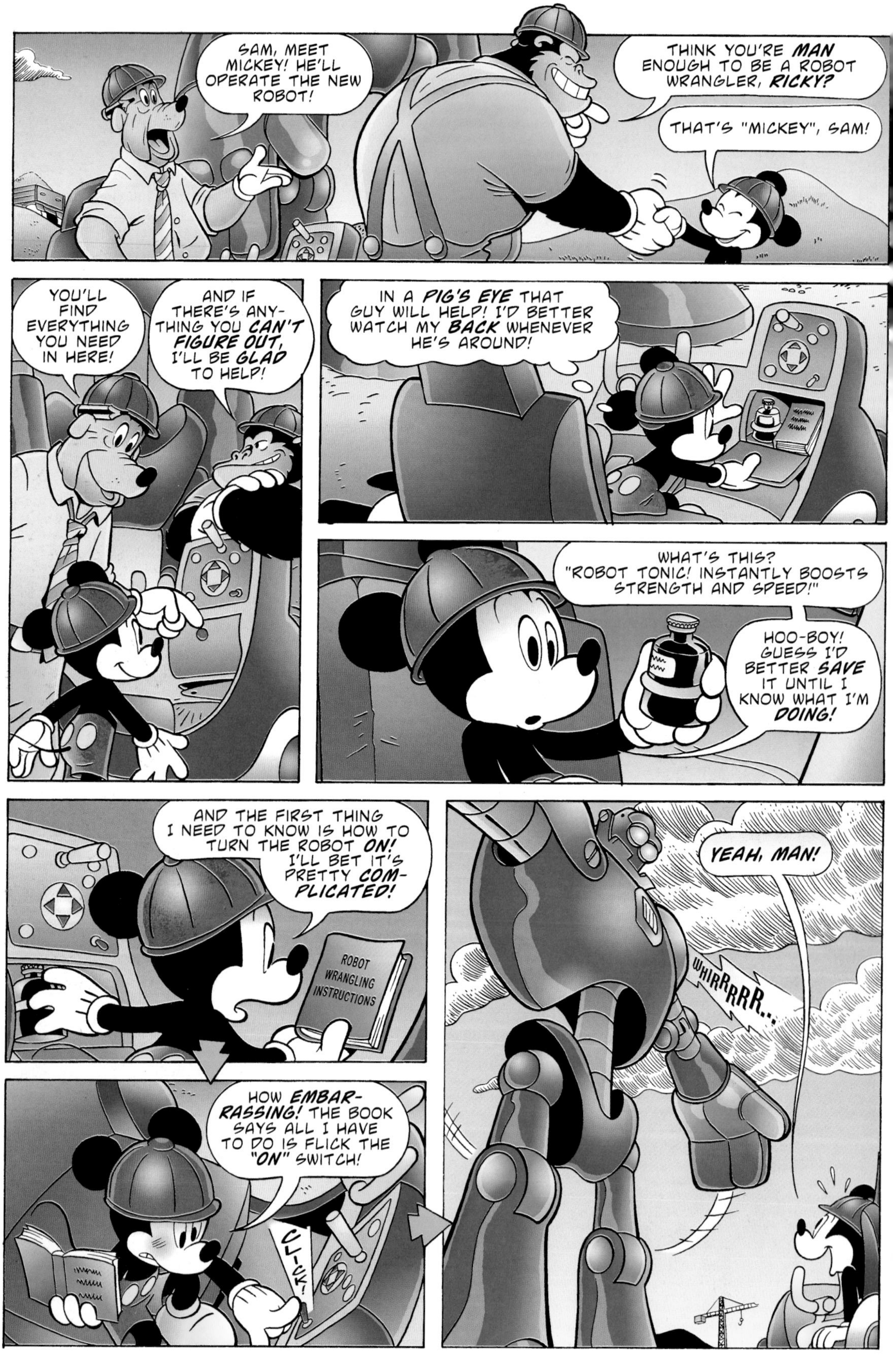
SAM, MEET MICKEY! HE'LL OPERATE THE NEW ROBOT!
THINK YOU'RE MAN ENOUGH TO BE A ROBOT WRANGLER, RICKY?
THAT'S "MICKEY", SAM!
YOU'LL FIND EVERYTHING YOU NEED IN HERE!
AND IF THERE'S ANY-THING YOU CAN'T FIGURE OUT, I'LL BE GLAD TO HELP!
IN A PIG'S EYE THAT GUY WILL HELP! I'D BETTER WATCH MY BACK WHENEVER HE'S AROUND!
WHAT'S THIS? "ROBOT TONIC! INSTANTLY BOOSTS STRENGTH AND SPEED!"
HOO-BOY! GUESS I'D BETTER SAVE IT UNTIL I KNOW WHAT I'M DOING!
AND THE FIRST THING I NEED TO KNOW IS HOW TO TURN THE ROBOT ON! I'LL BET IT'S PRETTY COM-PLICATED!
ROBOT WRANGLING INSTRUCTIONS
HOW EMBAR-RASSING! THE BOOK SAYS ALL I HAVE TO DO IS FLICK THE "ON" SWITCH!
CLICK!
YEAH, MAN!
WHIRRRRR...

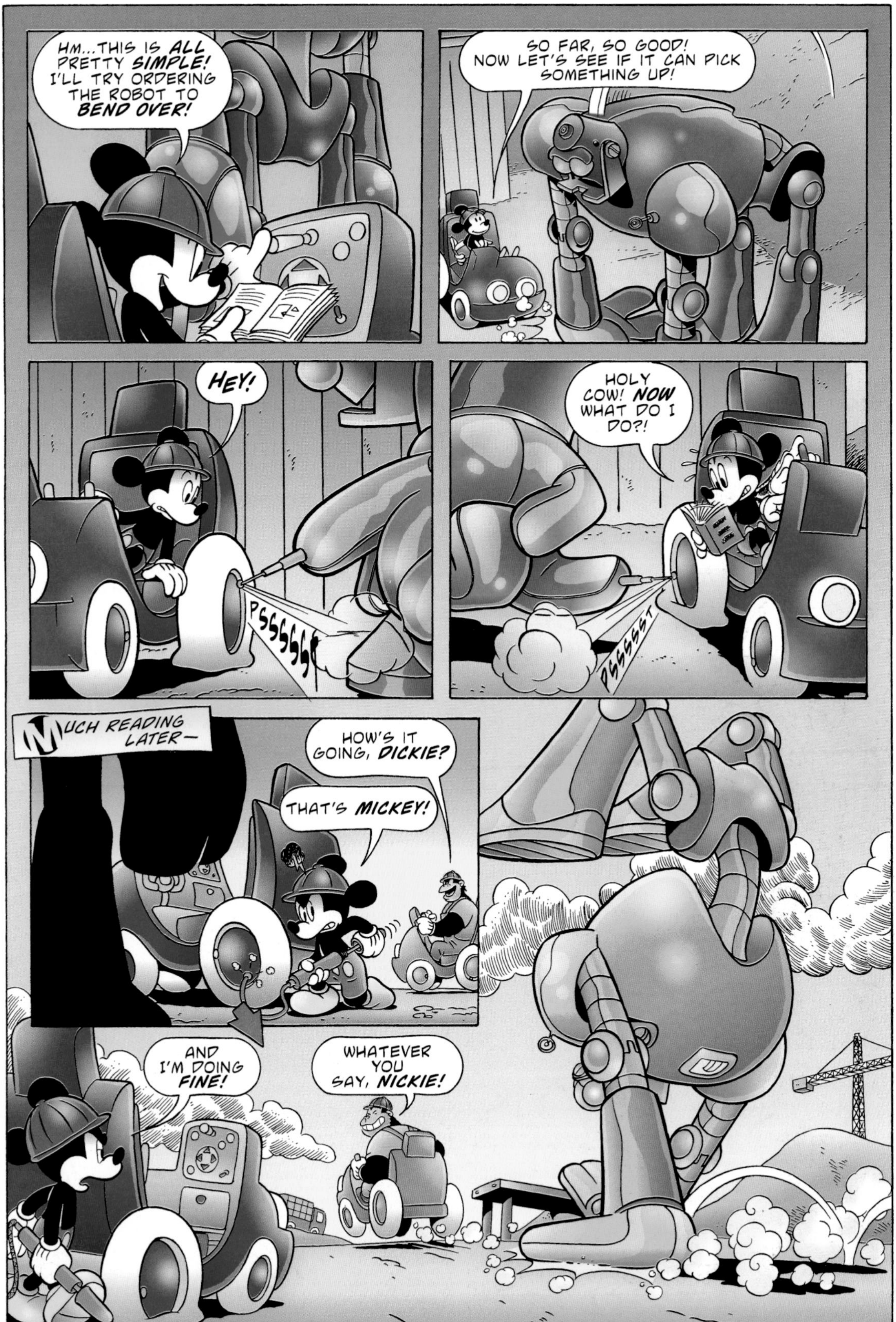
HM...THIS IS ALL PRETTY SIMPLE! I'LL TRY ORDERING THE ROBOT TO BEND OVER!
SO FAR, SO GOOD! NOW LET'S SEE IF IT CAN PICK SOMETHING UP!
HEY!
PSSSSSS
HOLY COW! NOW WHAT DO I DO?!
PSSSSST
MUCH READING LATER—
HOW'S IT GOING, DICKIE?
THAT'S MICKEY!
AND I'M DOING FINE!
WHATEVER YOU SAY, NICKIE!

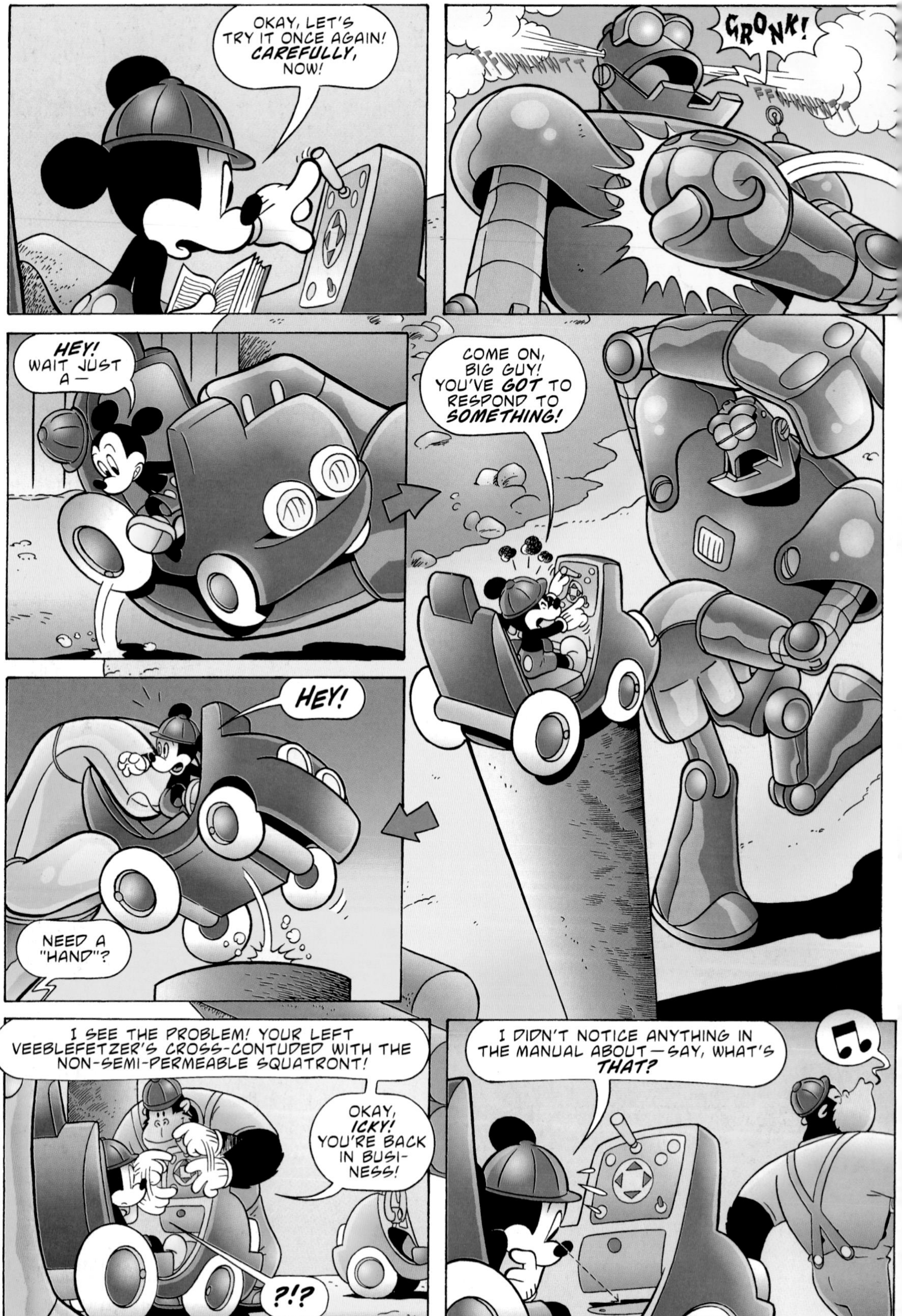

OKAY, LET'S TRY IT ONCE AGAIN! CAREFULLY, NOW!
GRONK!
HEY! WAIT JUST A—
COME ON, BIG GUY! YOU'VE GOT TO RESPOND TO SOMETHING!
HEY!
NEED A "HAND"?
I SEE THE PROBLEM! YOUR LEFT VEEBLEFETZER'S CROSS-CONTUDED WITH THE NON-SEMI-PERMEABLE SQUATRONT!
OKAY, ICKY! YOU'RE BACK IN BUSI-NESS!
?!?
I DIDN'T NOTICE ANYTHING IN THE MANUAL ABOUT—SAY, WHAT'S THAT?

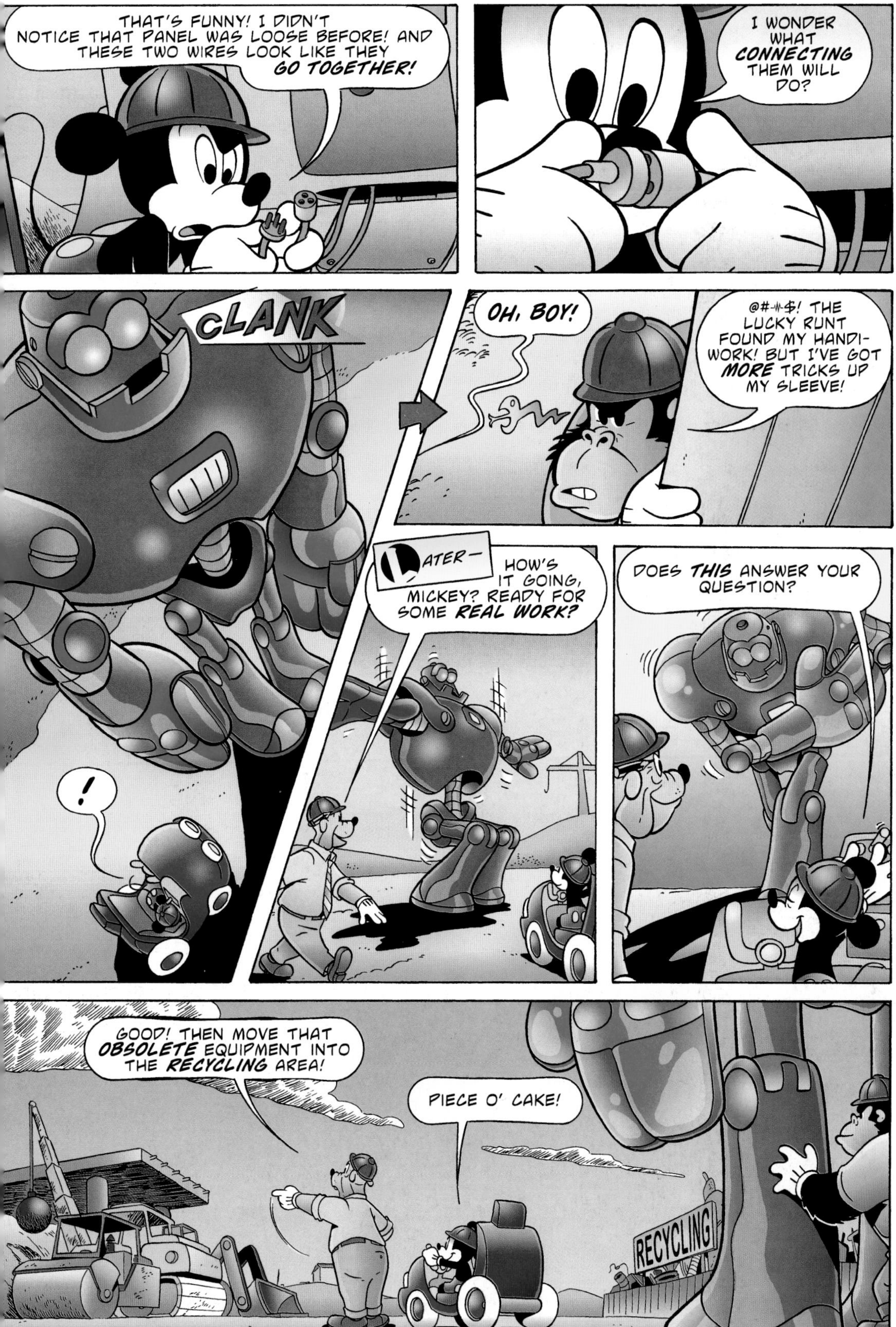
THAT'S FUNNY! I DIDN'T NOTICE THAT PANEL WAS LOOSE BEFORE! AND THESE TWO WIRES LOOK LIKE THEY GO TOGETHER!
I WONDER WHAT CONNECTING THEM WILL DO?
CLANK
!
OH, BOY!
@#-#-$! THE LUCKY RUNT FOUND MY HANDIWORK! BUT I'VE GOT MORE TRICKS UP MY SLEEVE!
LATER—
HOW'S IT GOING, MICKEY? READY FOR SOME REAL WORK?
DOES THIS ANSWER YOUR QUESTION?
GOOD! THEN MOVE THAT OBSOLETE EQUIPMENT INTO THE RECYCLING AREA!
PIECE O' CAKE!
RECYCLING

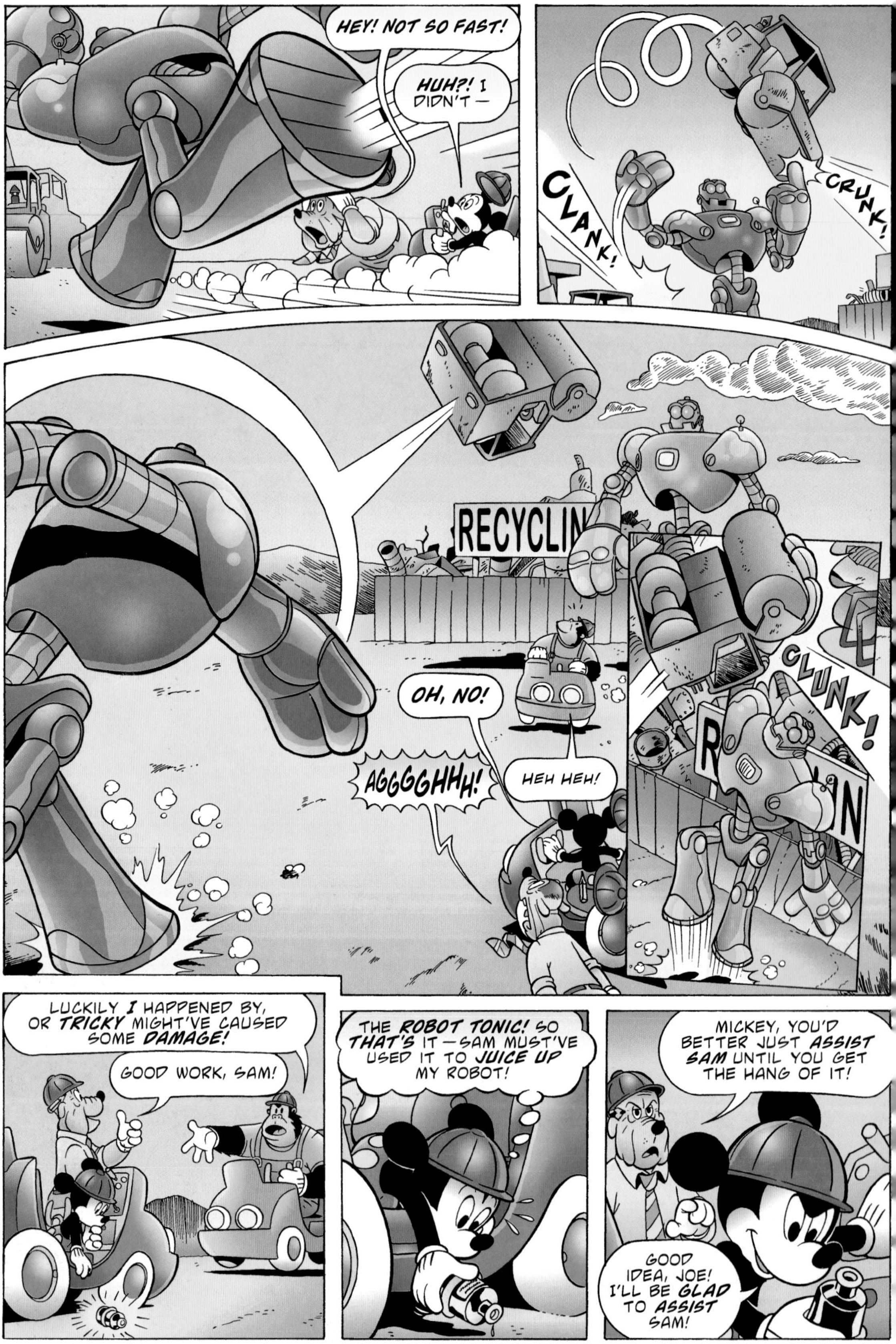
HEY! NOT SO FAST!
HUH?! I DIDN'T —
CLANK!
CRUNK!
RECYCLIN
OH, NO!
HEH HEH!
AGGGGHHH!
CLUNK!
LUCKILY I HAPPENED BY, OR TRICKY MIGHT'VE CAUSED SOME DAMAGE!
GOOD WORK, SAM!
THE ROBOT TONIC! SO THAT'S IT — SAM MUST'VE USED IT TO JUICE UP MY ROBOT!
MICKEY, YOU'D BETTER JUST ASSIST SAM UNTIL YOU GET THE HANG OF IT!
GOOD IDEA, JOE! I'LL BE GLAD TO ASSIST SAM!

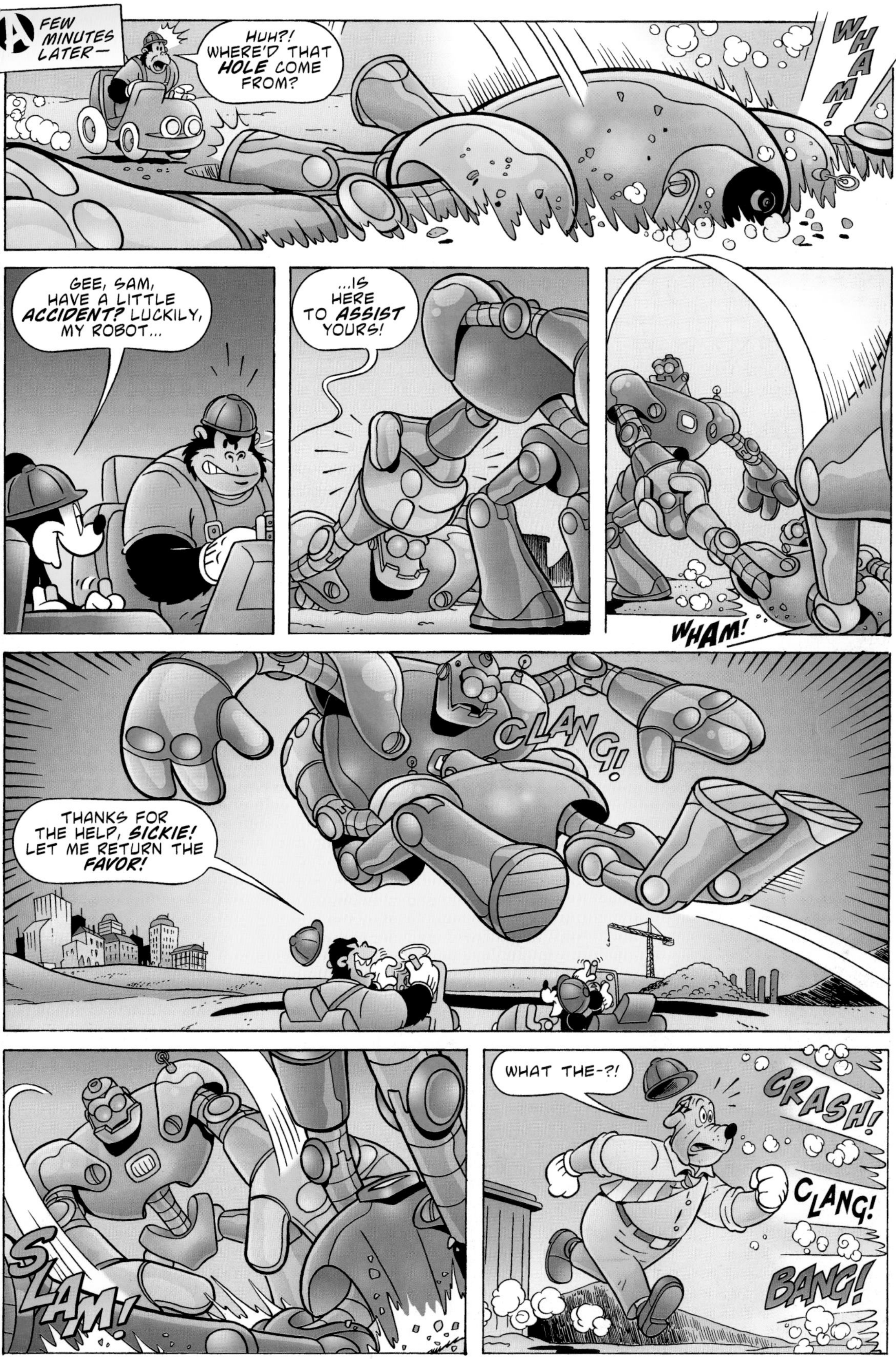
A FEW MINUTES LATER—
HUH?! WHERE'D THAT HOLE COME FROM?
WHAM!
GEE, SAM, HAVE A LITTLE ACCIDENT? LUCKILY, MY ROBOT...
...IS HERE TO ASSIST YOURS!
WHAM!
CLANG!
THANKS FOR THE HELP, SICKIE! LET ME RETURN THE FAVOR!
SLAM!
WHAT THE-?!
CRASH!
CLANG!
BANG!

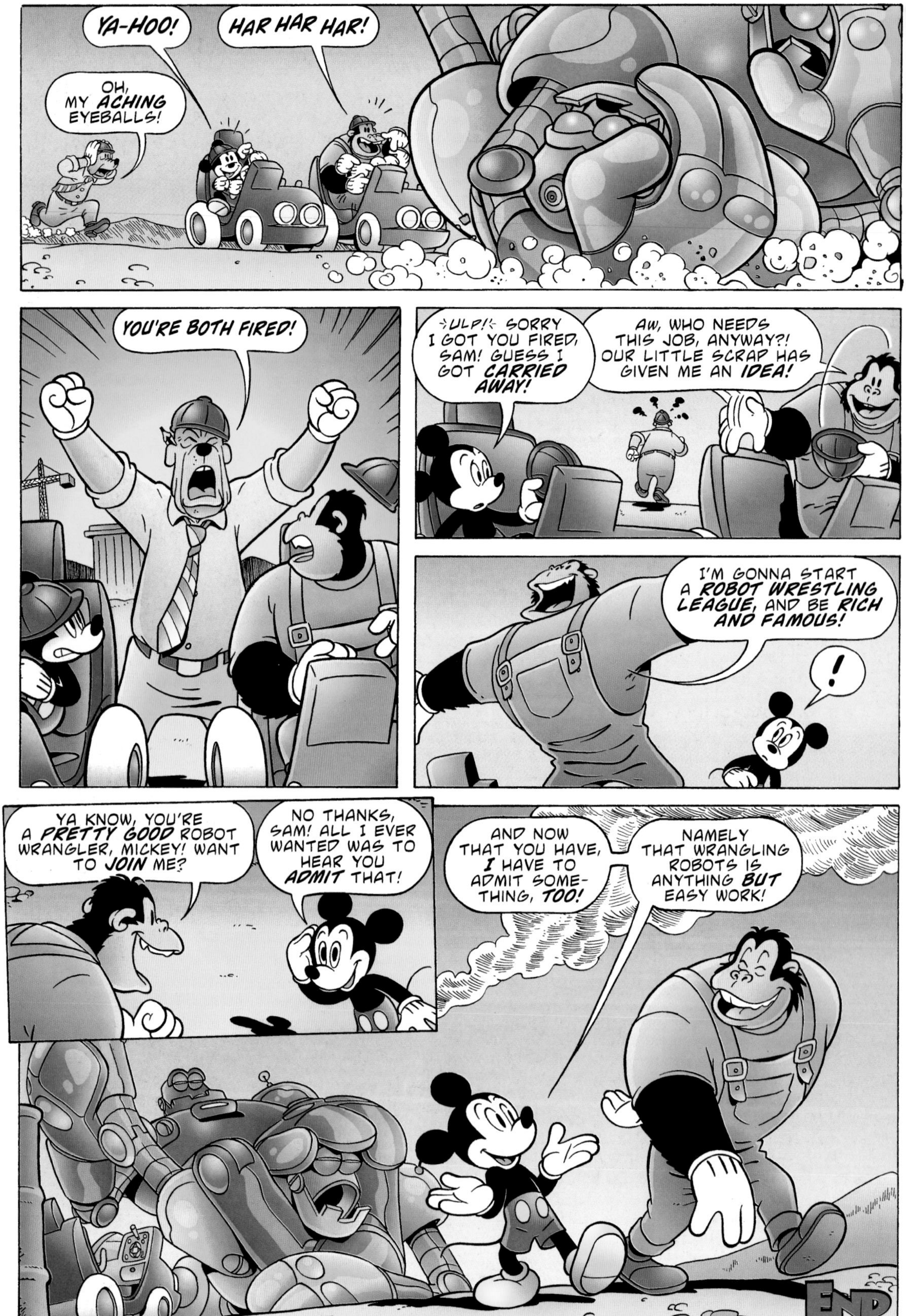
YA-HOO!
HAR HAR HAR!
OH, MY ACHING EYEBALLS!
YOU'RE BOTH FIRED!
ULP! SORRY I GOT YOU FIRED, SAM! GUESS I GOT CARRIED AWAY!
AW, WHO NEEDS THIS JOB, ANYWAY?! OUR LITTLE SCRAP HAS GIVEN ME AN IDEA!
I'M GONNA START A ROBOT WRESTLING LEAGUE, AND BE RICH AND FAMOUS!
!
YA KNOW, YOU'RE A PRETTY GOOD ROBOT WRANGLER, MICKEY! WANT TO JOIN ME?
NO THANKS, SAM! ALL I EVER WANTED WAS TO HEAR YOU ADMIT THAT!
AND NOW THAT YOU HAVE, I HAVE TO ADMIT SOME-THING, TOO!
NAMELY THAT WRANGLING ROBOTS IS ANYTHING BUT EASY WORK!
END

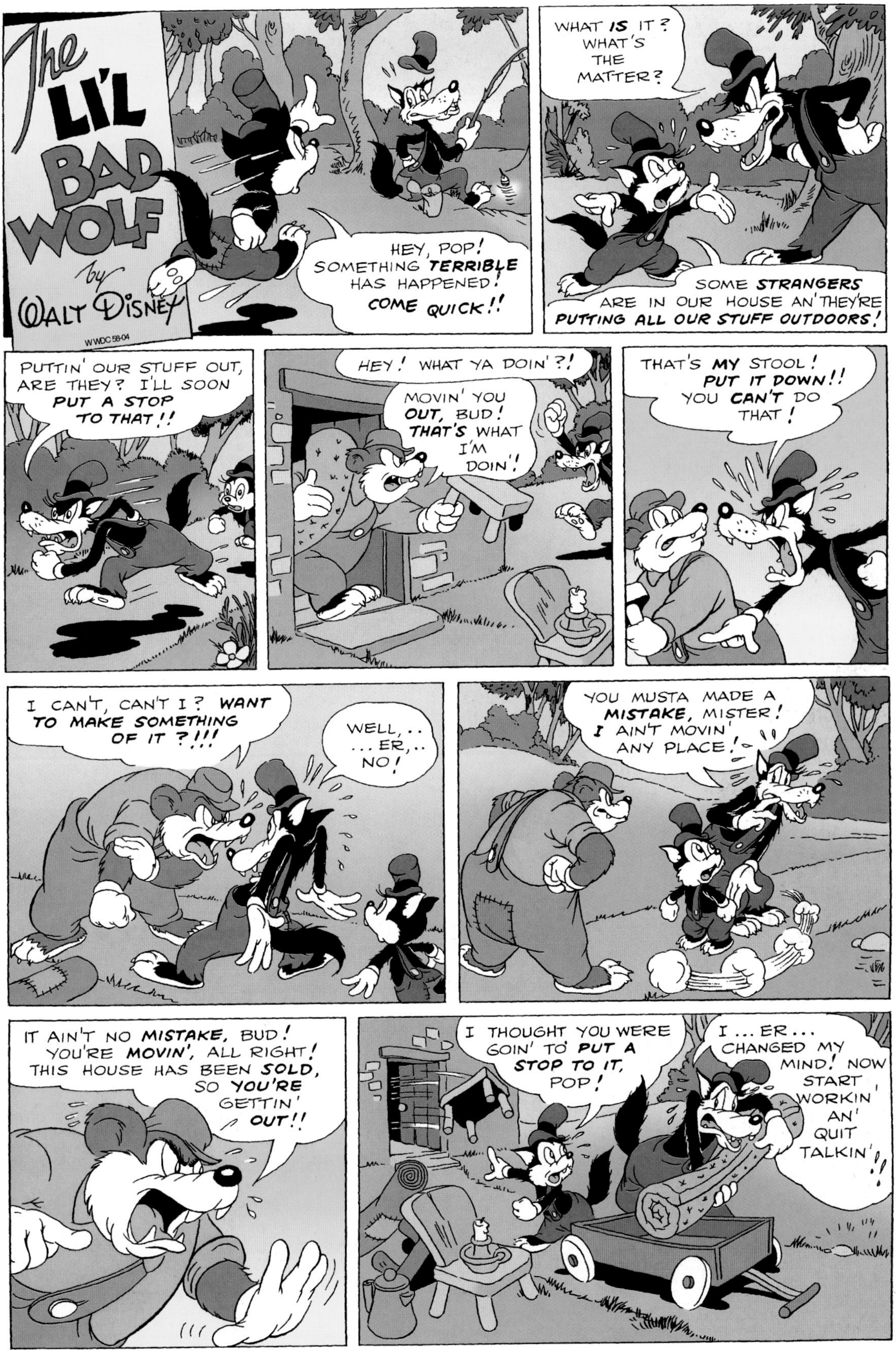
The LI'L BAD WOLF
by WALT DISNEY
WWDC 58-04
HEY, POP! SOMETHING TERRIBLE HAS HAPPENED! COME QUICK!!
WHAT IS IT? WHAT'S THE MATTER?
SOME STRANGERS ARE IN OUR HOUSE AN' THEY'RE PUTTING ALL OUR STUFF OUTDOORS!
PUTTIN' OUR STUFF OUT, ARE THEY? I'LL SOON PUT A STOP TO THAT!!
HEY! WHAT YA DOIN'?!
MOVIN' YOU OUT, BUD! THAT'S WHAT I'M DOIN'!
THAT'S MY STOOL! PUT IT DOWN!! YOU CAN'T DO THAT!
I CAN'T, CAN'T I? WANT TO MAKE SOMETHING OF IT?!!!
WELL, ... ER, .. NO!
YOU MUSTA MADE A MISTAKE, MISTER! I AIN'T MOVIN' ANY PLACE!
IT AIN'T NO MISTAKE, BUD! YOU'RE MOVIN', ALL RIGHT! THIS HOUSE HAS BEEN SOLD, SO YOU'RE GETTIN' OUT!!
I THOUGHT YOU WERE GOIN' TO PUT A STOP TO IT, POP!
I ... ER ... CHANGED MY MIND! NOW START WORKIN' AN' QUIT TALKIN'!!

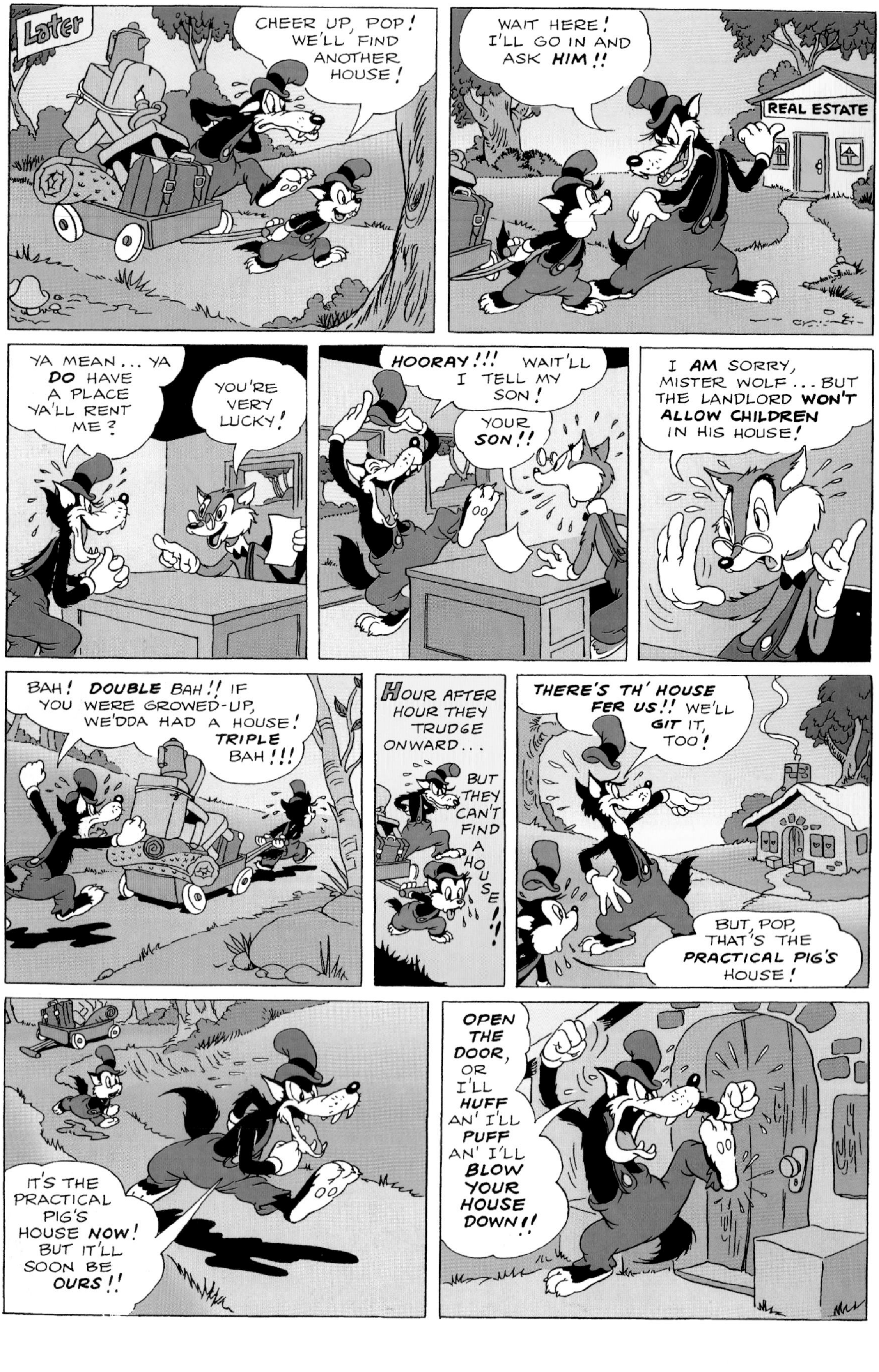
Later
CHEER UP, POP! WE'LL FIND ANOTHER HOUSE!
WAIT HERE! I'LL GO IN AND ASK HIM!!
REAL ESTATE
YA MEAN... YA DO HAVE A PLACE YA'LL RENT ME?
YOU'RE VERY LUCKY!
HOORAY!!! WAIT'LL I TELL MY SON!
YOUR SON!!
I AM SORRY, MISTER WOLF... BUT THE LANDLORD WON'T ALLOW CHILDREN IN HIS HOUSE!
BAH! DOUBLE BAH!! IF YOU WERE GROWED-UP, WE'DDA HAD A HOUSE! TRIPLE BAH!!!
HOUR AFTER HOUR THEY TRUDGE ONWARD...
BUT THEY CAN'T FIND A HOUSE!!
THERE'S TH' HOUSE FER US!! WE'LL GIT IT, TOO!
BUT, POP, THAT'S THE PRACTICAL PIG'S HOUSE!
IT'S THE PRACTICAL PIG'S HOUSE NOW! BUT IT'LL SOON BE OURS!!
OPEN THE DOOR, OR I'LL HUFF AN' I'LL PUFF AN' I'LL BLOW YOUR HOUSE DOWN!!

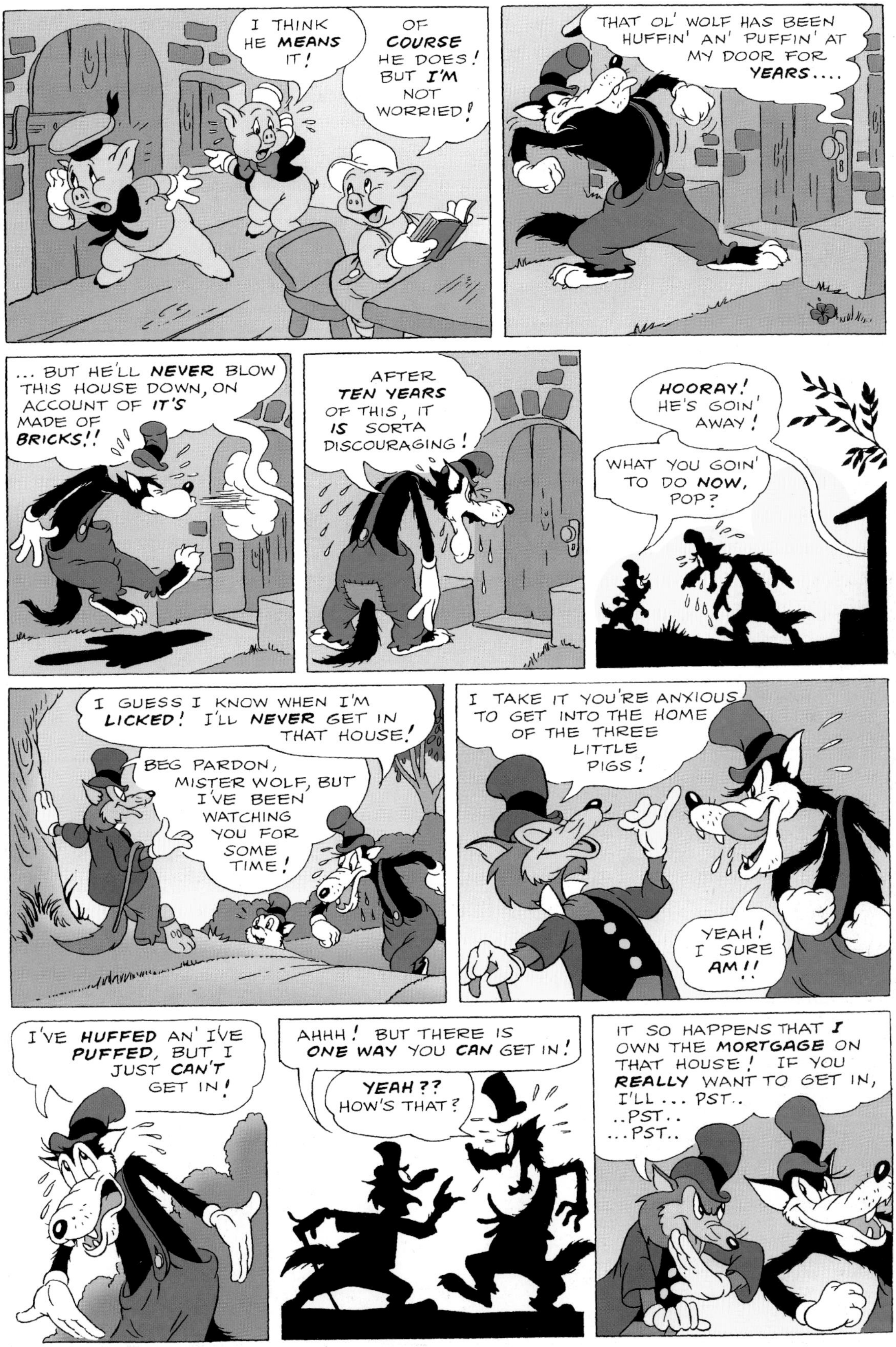
I THINK HE MEANS IT!
OF COURSE HE DOES! BUT I'M NOT WORRIED!
THAT OL' WOLF HAS BEEN HUFFIN' AN' PUFFIN' AT MY DOOR FOR YEARS....
... BUT HE'LL NEVER BLOW THIS HOUSE DOWN, ON ACCOUNT OF IT'S MADE OF BRICKS!!
AFTER TEN YEARS OF THIS, IT IS SORTA DISCOURAGING!
HOORAY! HE'S GOIN' AWAY!
WHAT YOU GOIN' TO DO NOW, POP?
I GUESS I KNOW WHEN I'M LICKED! I'LL NEVER GET IN THAT HOUSE!
BEG PARDON, MISTER WOLF, BUT I'VE BEEN WATCHING YOU FOR SOME TIME!
I TAKE IT YOU'RE ANXIOUS TO GET INTO THE HOME OF THE THREE LITTLE PIGS!
YEAH! I SURE AM!!
I'VE HUFFED AN' I'VE PUFFED, BUT I JUST CAN'T GET IN!
AHHH! BUT THERE IS ONE WAY YOU CAN GET IN!
YEAH?? HOW'S THAT?
IT SO HAPPENS THAT I OWN THE MORTGAGE ON THAT HOUSE! IF YOU REALLY WANT TO GET IN, I'LL ... PST.. ..PST.. ...PST..

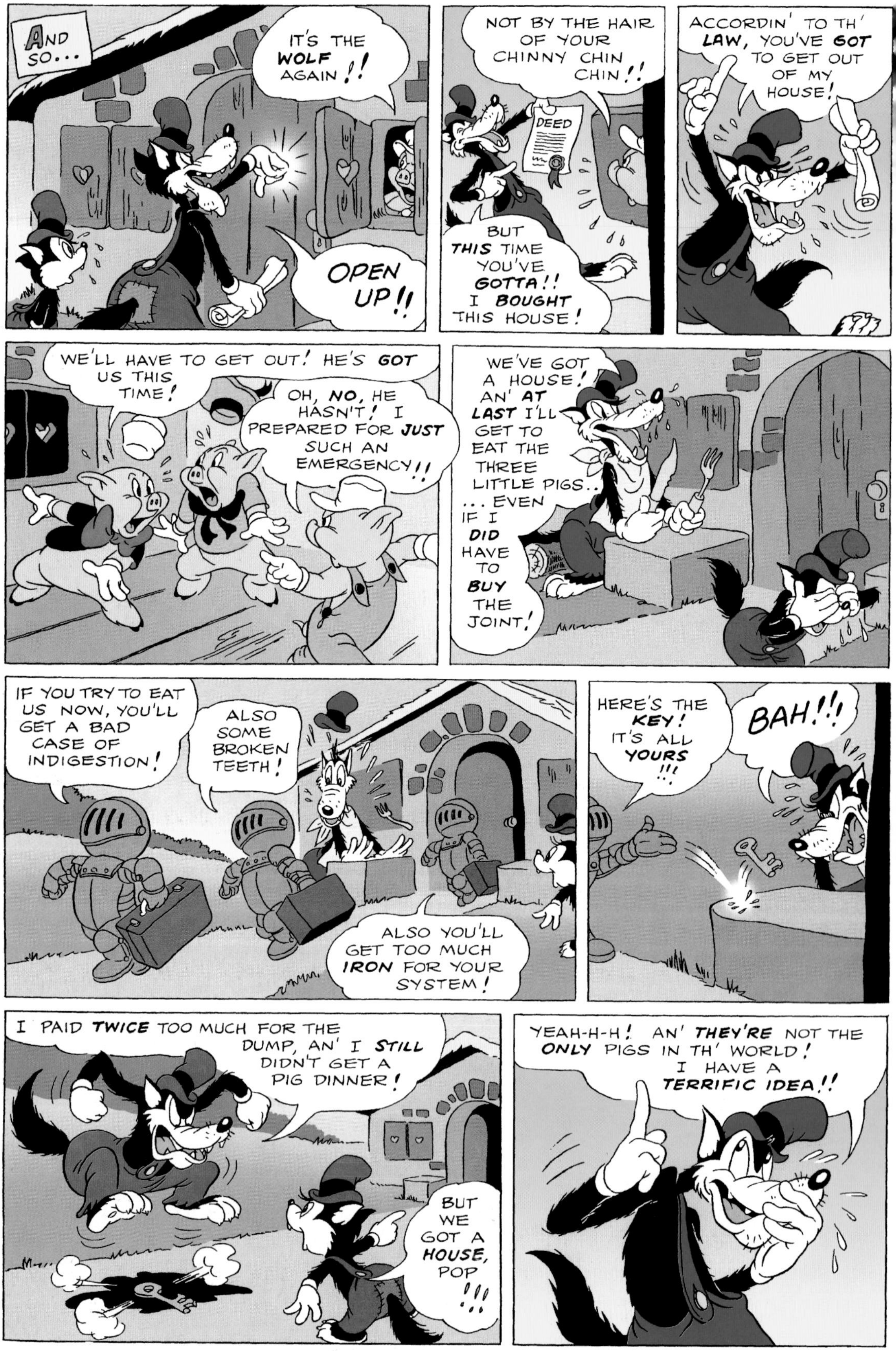

AND SO...
IT'S THE WOLF AGAIN !!
OPEN UP !!
NOT BY THE HAIR OF YOUR CHINNY CHIN CHIN !!
DEED
BUT THIS TIME YOU'VE GOTTA !! I BOUGHT THIS HOUSE !
ACCORDIN' TO TH' LAW, YOU'VE GOT TO GET OUT OF MY HOUSE !
WE'LL HAVE TO GET OUT ! HE'S GOT US THIS TIME !
OH, NO, HE HASN'T ! I PREPARED FOR JUST SUCH AN EMERGENCY !!
WE'VE GOT A HOUSE ! AN' AT LAST I'LL GET TO EAT THE THREE LITTLE PIGS... EVEN IF I DID HAVE TO BUY THE JOINT !
IF YOU TRY TO EAT US NOW, YOU'LL GET A BAD CASE OF INDIGESTION !
ALSO SOME BROKEN TEETH !
ALSO YOU'LL GET TOO MUCH IRON FOR YOUR SYSTEM !
HERE'S THE KEY ! IT'S ALL YOURS !!!
BAH !!!
I PAID TWICE TOO MUCH FOR THE DUMP, AN' I STILL DIDN'T GET A PIG DINNER !
BUT WE GOT A HOUSE, POP !!!
YEAH-H-H ! AN' THEY'RE NOT THE ONLY PIGS IN TH' WORLD ! I HAVE A TERRIFIC IDEA !!

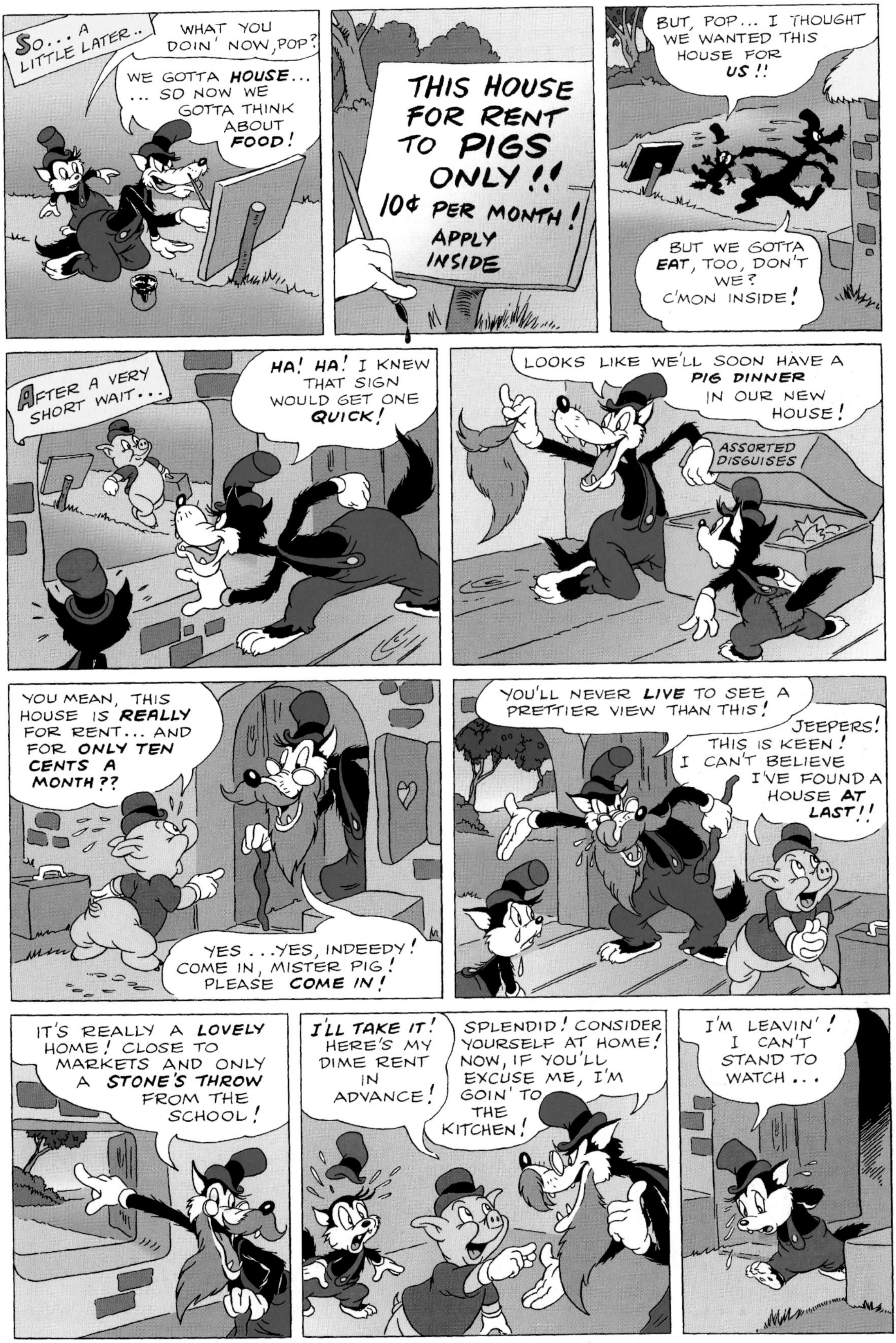

SO... A LITTLE LATER..
WHAT YOU DOIN' NOW, POP?
WE GOTTA HOUSE... ... SO NOW WE GOTTA THINK ABOUT FOOD!
THIS HOUSE FOR RENT TO PIGS ONLY!! 10¢ PER MONTH! APPLY INSIDE
BUT, POP... I THOUGHT WE WANTED THIS HOUSE FOR US!!
BUT WE GOTTA EAT, TOO, DON'T WE? C'MON INSIDE!
AFTER A VERY SHORT WAIT...
HA! HA! I KNEW THAT SIGN WOULD GET ONE QUICK!
LOOKS LIKE WE'LL SOON HAVE A PIG DINNER IN OUR NEW HOUSE!
ASSORTED DISGUISES
YOU MEAN, THIS HOUSE IS REALLY FOR RENT... AND FOR ONLY TEN CENTS A MONTH??
YES...YES, INDEEDY! COME IN, MISTER PIG! PLEASE COME IN!
YOU'LL NEVER LIVE TO SEE A PRETTIER VIEW THAN THIS!
JEEPERS! THIS IS KEEN! I CAN'T BELIEVE I'VE FOUND A HOUSE AT LAST!!
IT'S REALLY A LOVELY HOME! CLOSE TO MARKETS AND ONLY A STONE'S THROW FROM THE SCHOOL!
I'LL TAKE IT! HERE'S MY DIME RENT IN ADVANCE!
SPLENDID! CONSIDER YOURSELF AT HOME! NOW, IF YOU'LL EXCUSE ME, I'M GOIN' TO THE KITCHEN!
I'M LEAVIN'! I CAN'T STAND TO WATCH...

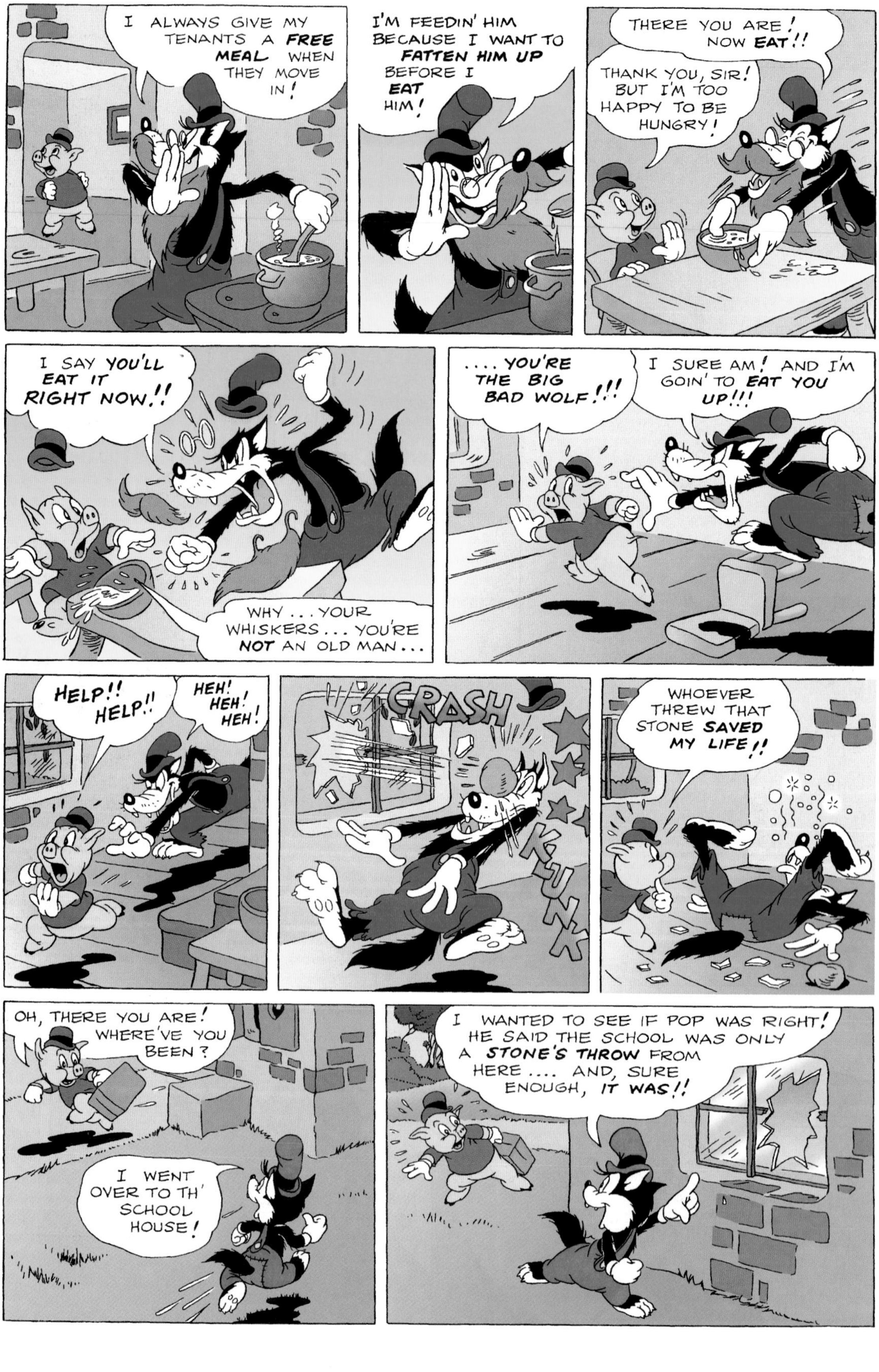
I ALWAYS GIVE MY TENANTS A FREE MEAL WHEN THEY MOVE IN!
I'M FEEDIN' HIM BECAUSE I WANT TO FATTEN HIM UP BEFORE I EAT HIM!
THERE YOU ARE! NOW EAT!!
THANK YOU, SIR! BUT I'M TOO HAPPY TO BE HUNGRY!
I SAY YOU'LL EAT IT RIGHT NOW!!
WHY ... YOUR WHISKERS ... YOU'RE NOT AN OLD MAN ...
.... YOU'RE THE BIG BAD WOLF!!!
I SURE AM! AND I'M GOIN' TO EAT YOU UP!!!
HELP!! HELP!!
HEH! HEH! HEH!
CRASH
KLUNK
WHOEVER THREW THAT STONE SAVED MY LIFE!!
OH, THERE YOU ARE! WHERE'VE YOU BEEN?
I WENT OVER TO TH' SCHOOL HOUSE!
I WANTED TO SEE IF POP WAS RIGHT! HE SAID THE SCHOOL WAS ONLY A STONE'S THROW FROM HERE .... AND, SURE ENOUGH, IT WAS!!

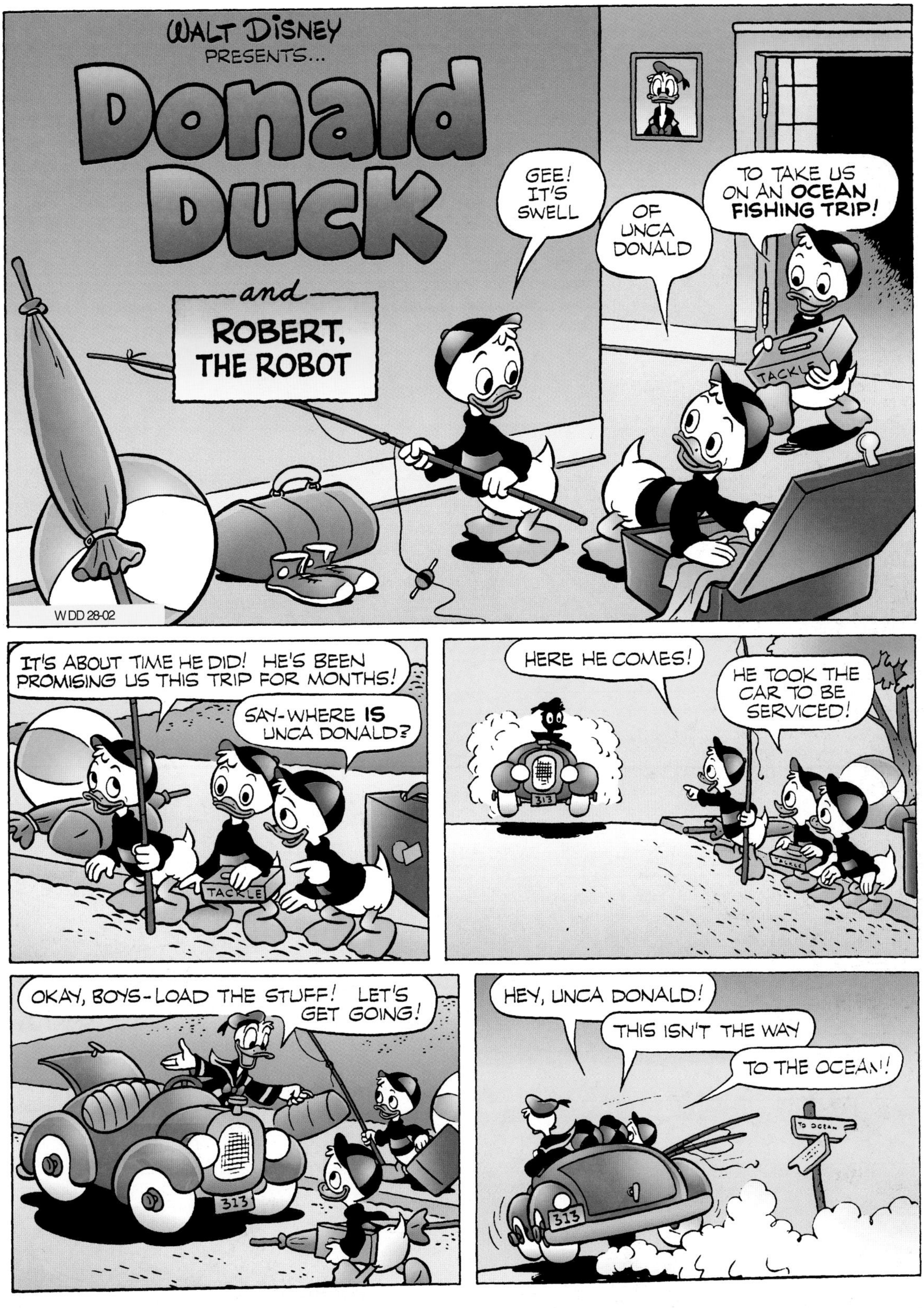

WALT DISNEY
PRESENTS...
Donald Duck
and
ROBERT, THE ROBOT
GEE! IT'S SWELL
OF UNCA DONALD
TO TAKE US ON AN OCEAN FISHING TRIP!
TACKLE
WDD 28-02
IT'S ABOUT TIME HE DID! HE'S BEEN PROMISING US THIS TRIP FOR MONTHS!
SAY-WHERE IS UNCA DONALD?
TACKLE
HERE HE COMES!
HE TOOK THE CAR TO BE SERVICED!
313
OKAY, BOYS-LOAD THE STUFF! LET'S GET GOING!
313
HEY, UNCA DONALD!
THIS ISN'T THE WAY
TO THE OCEAN!
TO OCEAN
313

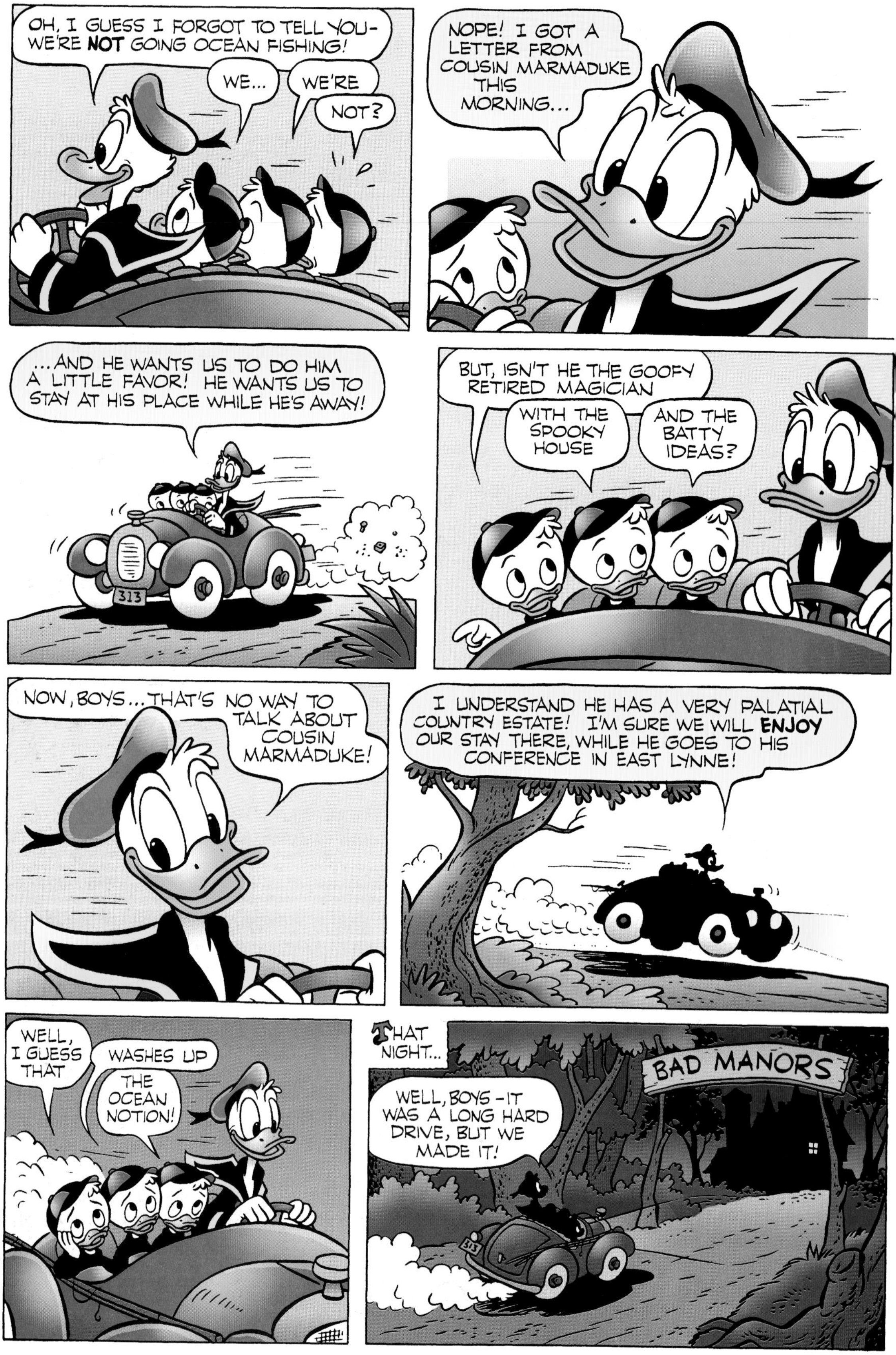
OH, I GUESS I FORGOT TO TELL YOU- WE'RE **NOT** GOING OCEAN FISHING!
WE...
WE'RE
NOT?
NOPE! I GOT A LETTER FROM COUSIN MARMADUKE THIS MORNING...
...AND HE WANTS US TO DO HIM A LITTLE FAVOR! HE WANTS US TO STAY AT HIS PLACE WHILE HE'S AWAY!
313
BUT, ISN'T HE THE GOOFY RETIRED MAGICIAN
WITH THE SPOOKY HOUSE
AND THE BATTY IDEAS?
NOW, BOYS... THAT'S NO WAY TO TALK ABOUT COUSIN MARMADUKE!
I UNDERSTAND HE HAS A VERY PALATIAL COUNTRY ESTATE! I'M SURE WE WILL **ENJOY** OUR STAY THERE, WHILE HE GOES TO HIS CONFERENCE IN EAST LYNNE!
WELL, I GUESS THAT
WASHES UP
THE OCEAN NOTION!
THAT NIGHT...
BAD MANORS
WELL, BOYS - IT WAS A LONG HARD DRIVE, BUT WE MADE IT!
313

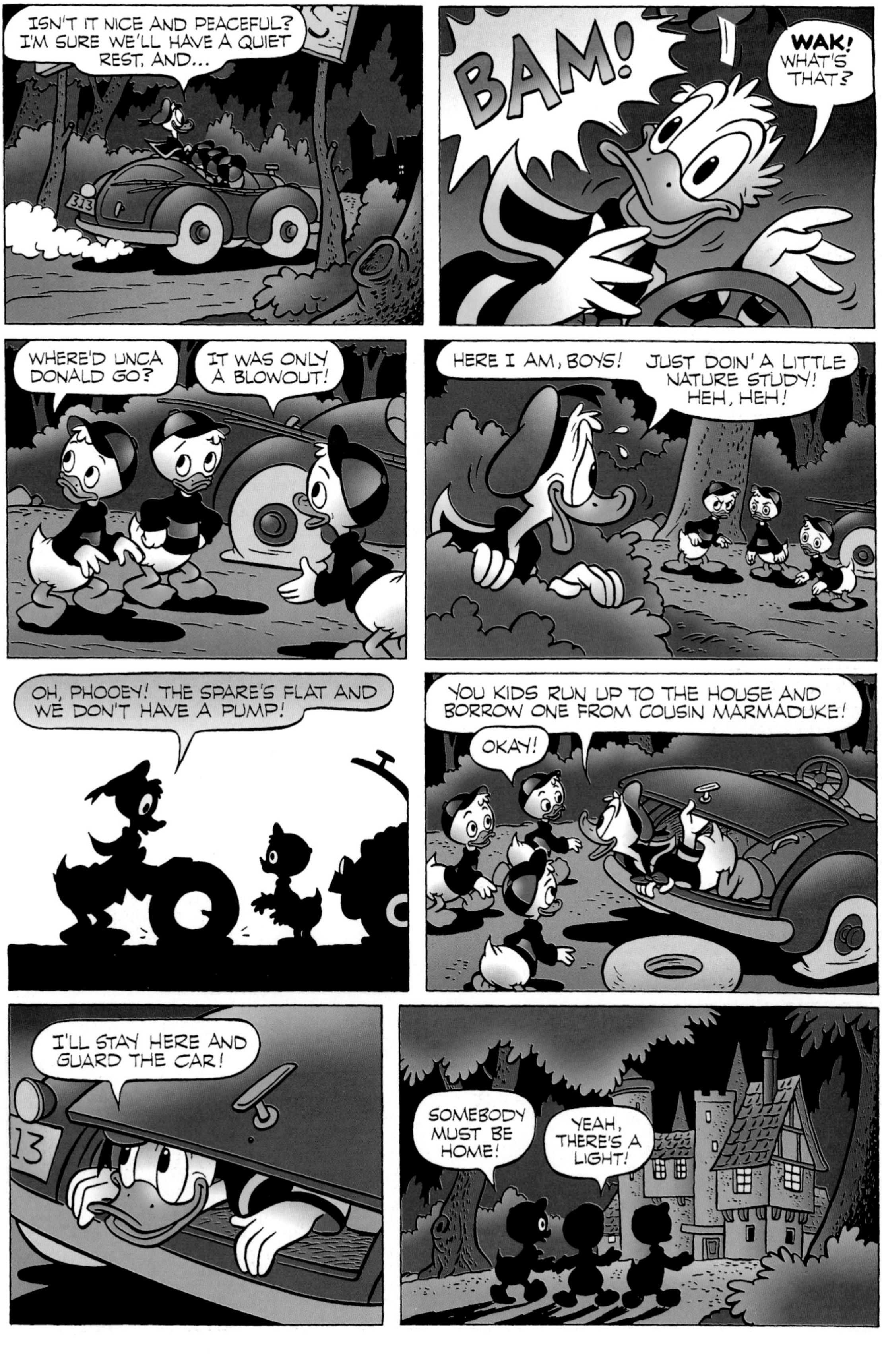
ISN'T IT NICE AND PEACEFUL? I'M SURE WE'LL HAVE A QUIET REST, AND...
313
BAM!
WAK! WHAT'S THAT?
WHERE'D UNCA DONALD GO?
IT WAS ONLY A BLOWOUT!
HERE I AM, BOYS!
JUST DOIN' A LITTLE NATURE STUDY! HEH, HEH!
OH, PHOOEY! THE SPARE'S FLAT AND WE DON'T HAVE A PUMP!
YOU KIDS RUN UP TO THE HOUSE AND BORROW ONE FROM COUSIN MARMADUKE!
OKAY!
I'LL STAY HERE AND GUARD THE CAR!
13
SOMEBODY MUST BE HOME!
YEAH, THERE'S A LIGHT!

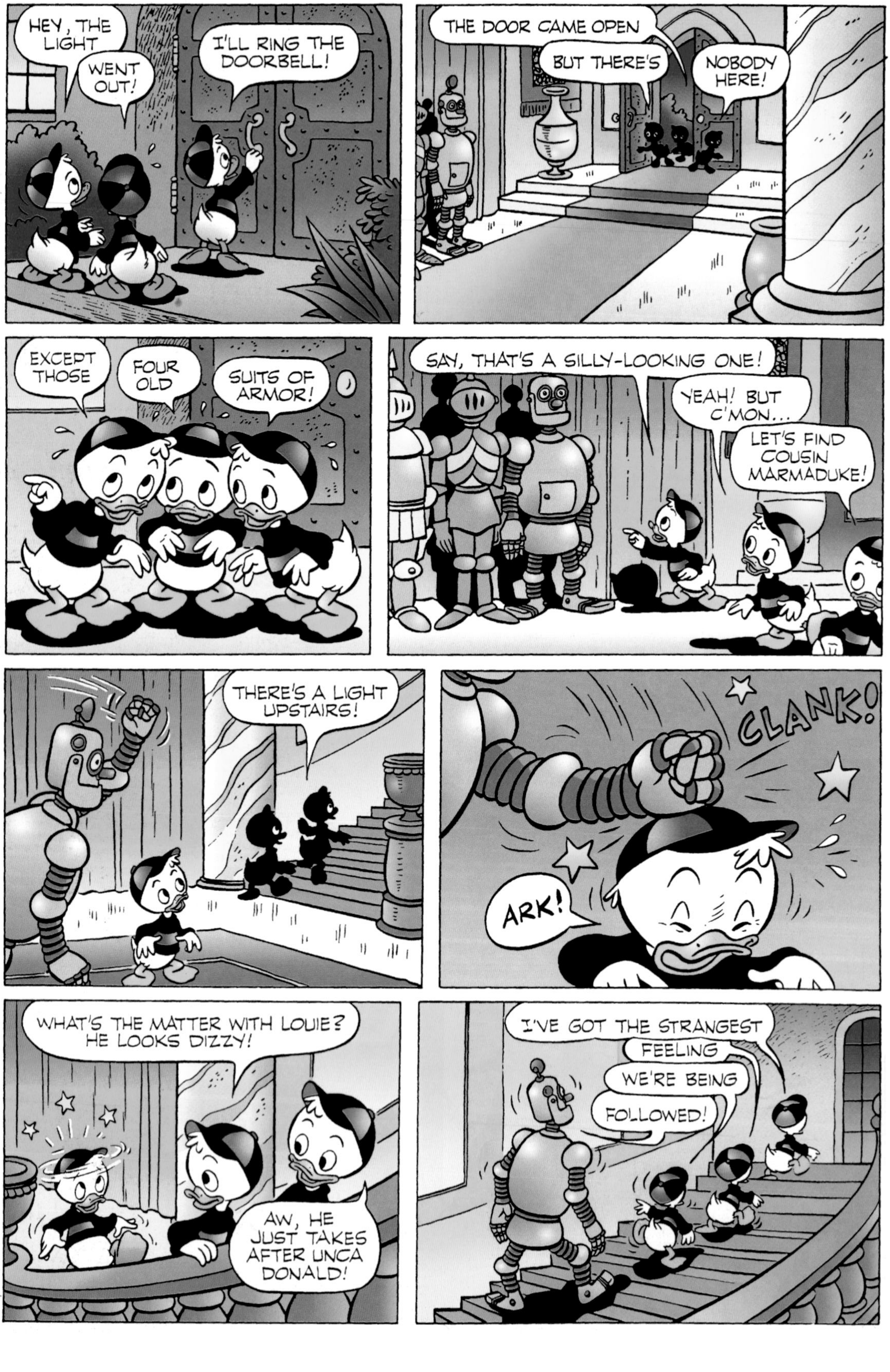
HEY, THE LIGHT
WENT OUT!
I'LL RING THE DOORBELL!
THE DOOR CAME OPEN
BUT THERE'S
NOBODY HERE!
EXCEPT THOSE
FOUR OLD
SUITS OF ARMOR!
SAY, THAT'S A SILLY-LOOKING ONE!
YEAH! BUT C'MON...
LET'S FIND COUSIN MARMADUKE!
THERE'S A LIGHT UPSTAIRS!
CLANK!
ARK!
WHAT'S THE MATTER WITH LOUIE? HE LOOKS DIZZY!
AW, HE JUST TAKES AFTER UNCA DONALD!
I'VE GOT THE STRANGEST
FEELING
WE'RE BEING
FOLLOWED!

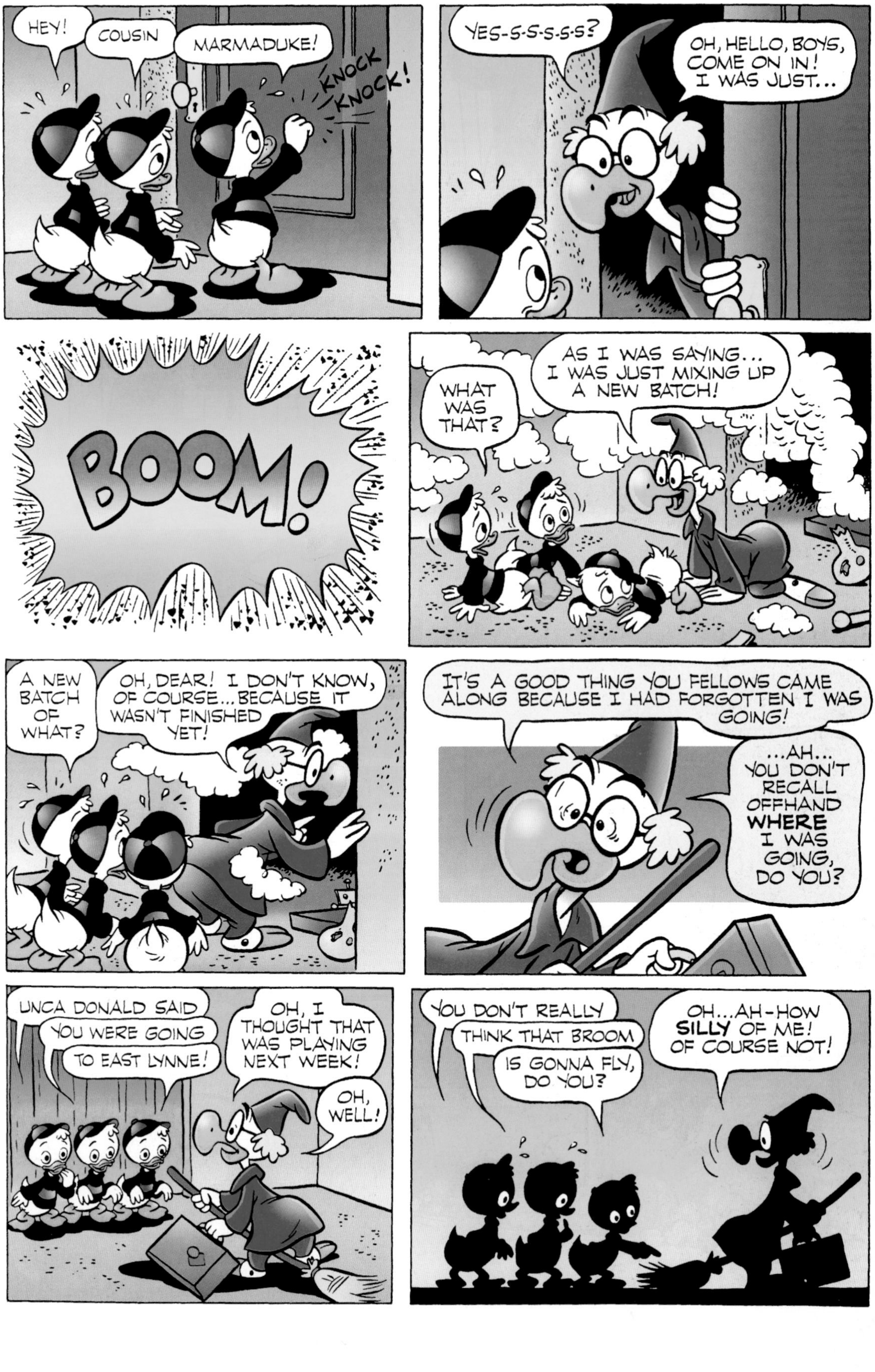
HEY!
COUSIN
MARMADUKE!
KNOCK KNOCK!
YES-S-S-S-S-S?
OH, HELLO, BOYS, COME ON IN! I WAS JUST...
BOOM!
WHAT WAS THAT?
AS I WAS SAYING... I WAS JUST MIXING UP A NEW BATCH!
A NEW BATCH OF WHAT?
OH, DEAR! I DON'T KNOW, OF COURSE... BECAUSE IT WASN'T FINISHED YET!
IT'S A GOOD THING YOU FELLOWS CAME ALONG BECAUSE I HAD FORGOTTEN I WAS GOING!
...AH... YOU DON'T RECALL OFFHAND WHERE I WAS GOING, DO YOU?
UNCA DONALD SAID
YOU WERE GOING
TO EAST LYNNE!
OH, I THOUGHT THAT WAS PLAYING NEXT WEEK!
OH, WELL!
YOU DON'T REALLY
THINK THAT BROOM
IS GONNA FLY, DO YOU?
OH...AH-HOW SILLY OF ME! OF COURSE NOT!

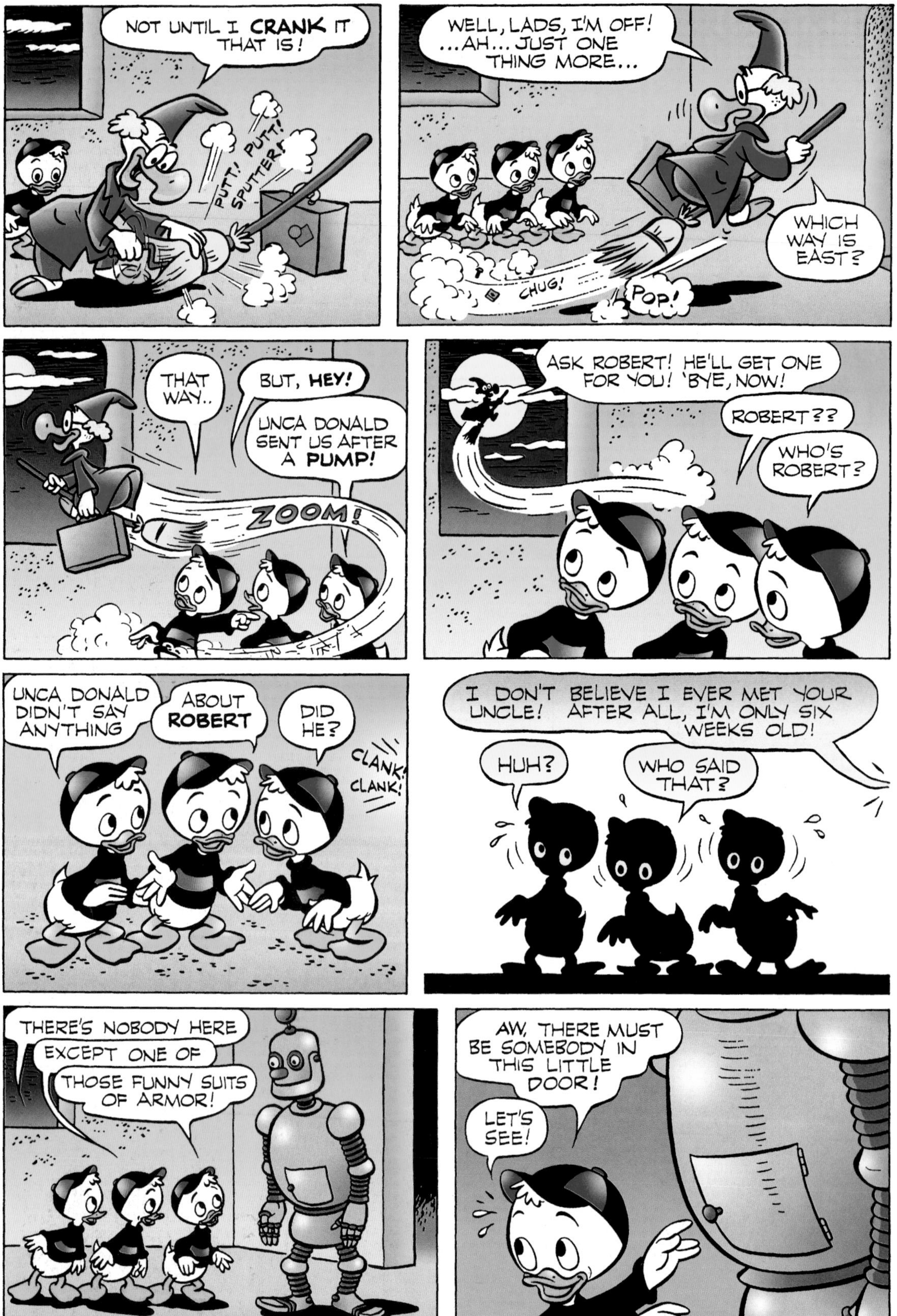
NOT UNTIL I **CRANK** IT THAT IS!
PUTT! PUTT! SPUTTER!
WELL, LADS, I'M OFF! ...AH... JUST ONE THING MORE...
WHICH WAY IS EAST?
CHUG!
POP!
THAT WAY..
BUT, **HEY!**
UNCA DONALD SENT US AFTER A **PUMP!**
ZOOM!
ASK ROBERT! HE'LL GET ONE FOR YOU! 'BYE, NOW!
ROBERT??
WHO'S ROBERT?
UNCA DONALD DIDN'T SAY ANYTHING
ABOUT **ROBERT**
DID HE?
CLANK! CLANK!
I DON'T BELIEVE I EVER MET YOUR UNCLE! AFTER ALL, I'M ONLY SIX WEEKS OLD!
HUH?
WHO SAID THAT?
THERE'S NOBODY HERE
EXCEPT ONE OF
THOSE FUNNY SUITS OF ARMOR!
AW, THERE MUST BE SOMEBODY IN THIS LITTLE DOOR!
LET'S SEE!

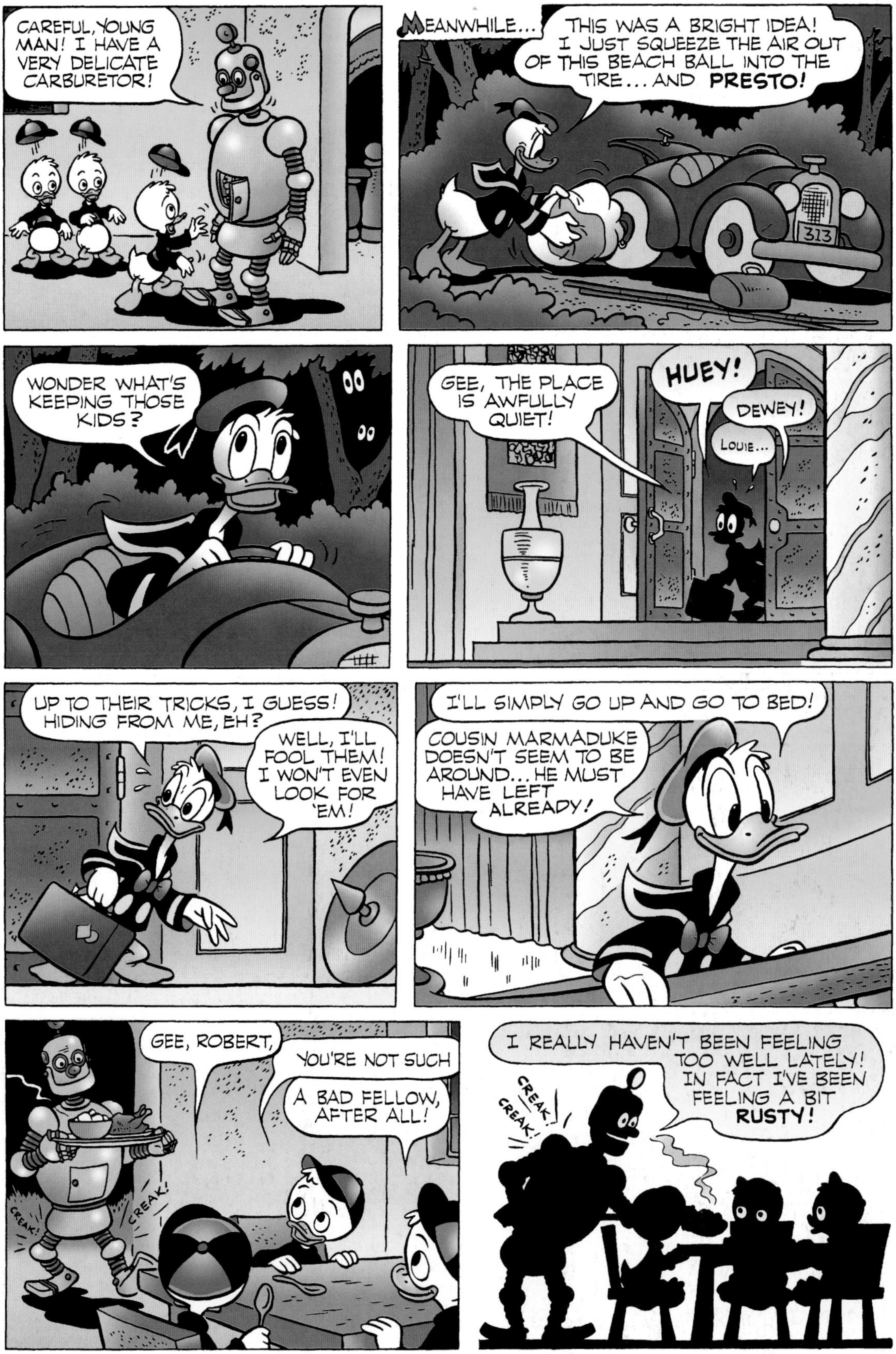
CAREFUL, YOUNG MAN! I HAVE A VERY DELICATE CARBURETOR!
MEANWHILE...
THIS WAS A BRIGHT IDEA! I JUST SQUEEZE THE AIR OUT OF THIS BEACH BALL INTO THE TIRE... AND PRESTO!
313
WONDER WHAT'S KEEPING THOSE KIDS?
GEE, THE PLACE IS AWFULLY QUIET!
HUEY!
DEWEY!
LOUIE...
UP TO THEIR TRICKS, I GUESS! HIDING FROM ME, EH?
WELL, I'LL FOOL THEM! I WON'T EVEN LOOK FOR 'EM!
I'LL SIMPLY GO UP AND GO TO BED!
COUSIN MARMADUKE DOESN'T SEEM TO BE AROUND... HE MUST HAVE LEFT ALREADY!
GEE, ROBERT,
YOU'RE NOT SUCH
A BAD FELLOW, AFTER ALL!
CREAK!
CREAK!
I REALLY HAVEN'T BEEN FEELING TOO WELL LATELY! IN FACT I'VE BEEN FEELING A BIT RUSTY!
CREAK!
CREAK!

RUSTY? OH, WE'LL FIX YOU UP!

WHERE'S YOUR OIL CAN?

WE'LL GIVE YOU A GOOD OIL JOB!

THE OIL CAN IS UPSTAIRS! I'LL GO GET IT WHILE YOU BOYS FINISH YOUR MILK!

I LIKE MILK, TOO, BUT IT RUSTS ME SOMETHING TERRIBLE!

SQUEAK!

SQUEAK!

HEY! MAYBE WE CAN STILL

GO OCEAN FISHING

IF ROBERT WILL HELP US!

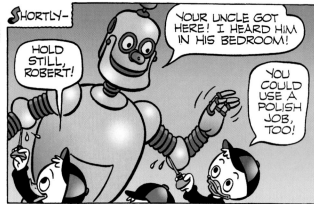

SHORTLY—

HOLD STILL, ROBERT!

YOUR UNCLE GOT HERE! I HEARD HIM IN HIS BEDROOM!

YOU COULD USE A POLISH JOB, TOO!

AND NOW, WE HAVE A FAVOR TO ASK OF YOU!

THE KIDS EXPLAIN THEIR PLIGHT TO A SYMPATHETIC ROBERT...

...SO YOU SEE, WE DIDN'T GET TO GO OCEAN FISHING!

BUT MAYBE YOU COULD **SCARE** UNCA DONALD AWAY

PURR-R-R

AND HE'D TAKE US!

I THINK WE CAN MANAGE IT! MARMADUKE HAS LOTS OF MAGICIAN'S STUFF HERE!

WE USED TO HAVE SOME **REAL** SPOOKS AROUND...BUT THEY GOT SCARED AND LEFT!

WE'LL GO TO BED, ROBERT

AND LEAVE

EVERYTHING TO YOU!

IS THAT YOU, BOYS?

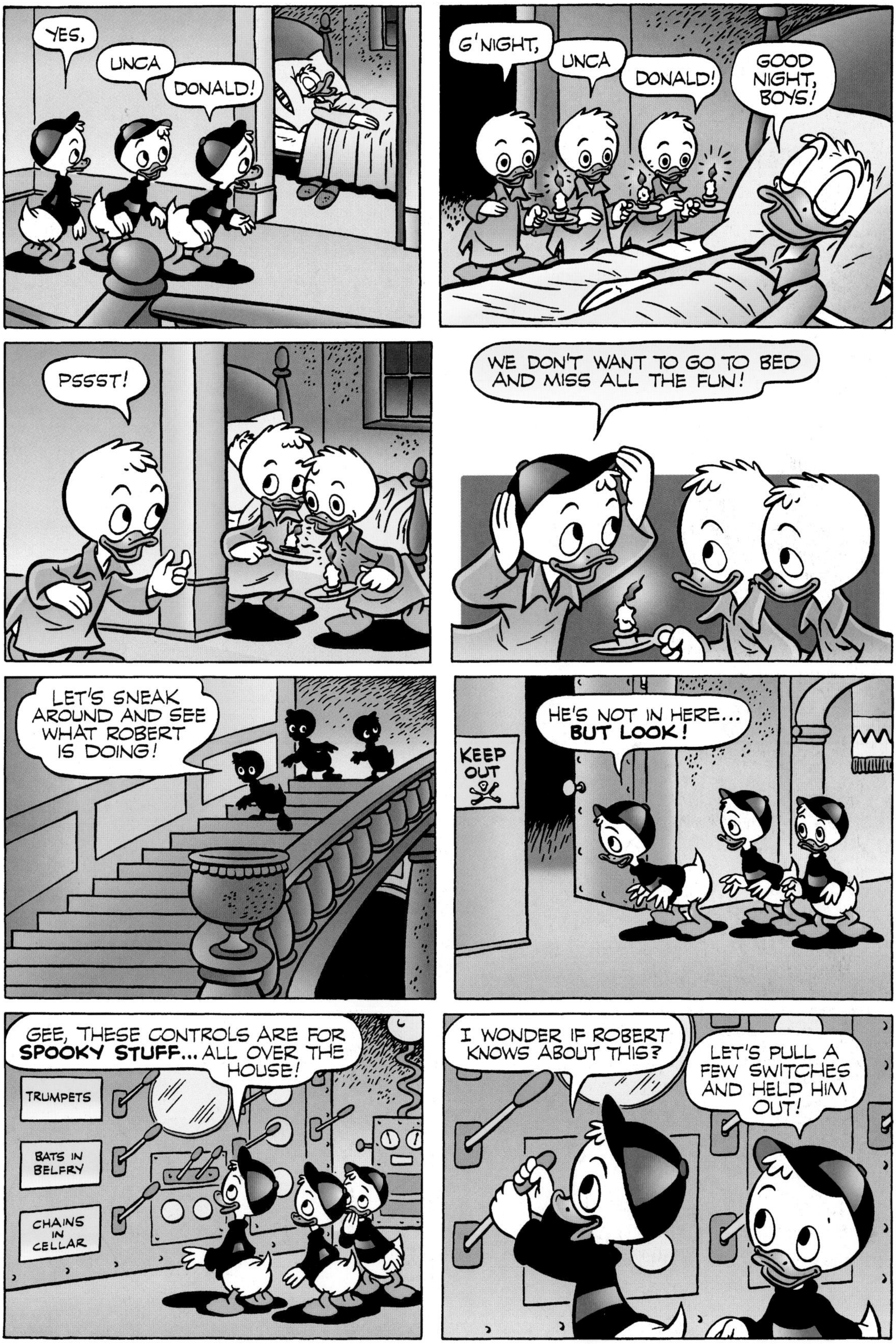
YES,
UNCA
DONALD!
G'NIGHT,
UNCA
DONALD!
GOOD NIGHT, BOYS!
PSSST!
WE DON'T WANT TO GO TO BED AND MISS ALL THE FUN!
LET'S SNEAK AROUND AND SEE WHAT ROBERT IS DOING!
KEEP OUT
HE'S NOT IN HERE... BUT LOOK!
GEE, THESE CONTROLS ARE FOR SPOOKY STUFF... ALL OVER THE HOUSE!
TRUMPETS
BATS IN BELFRY
CHAINS IN CELLAR
I WONDER IF ROBERT KNOWS ABOUT THIS?
LET'S PULL A FEW SWITCHES AND HELP HIM OUT!

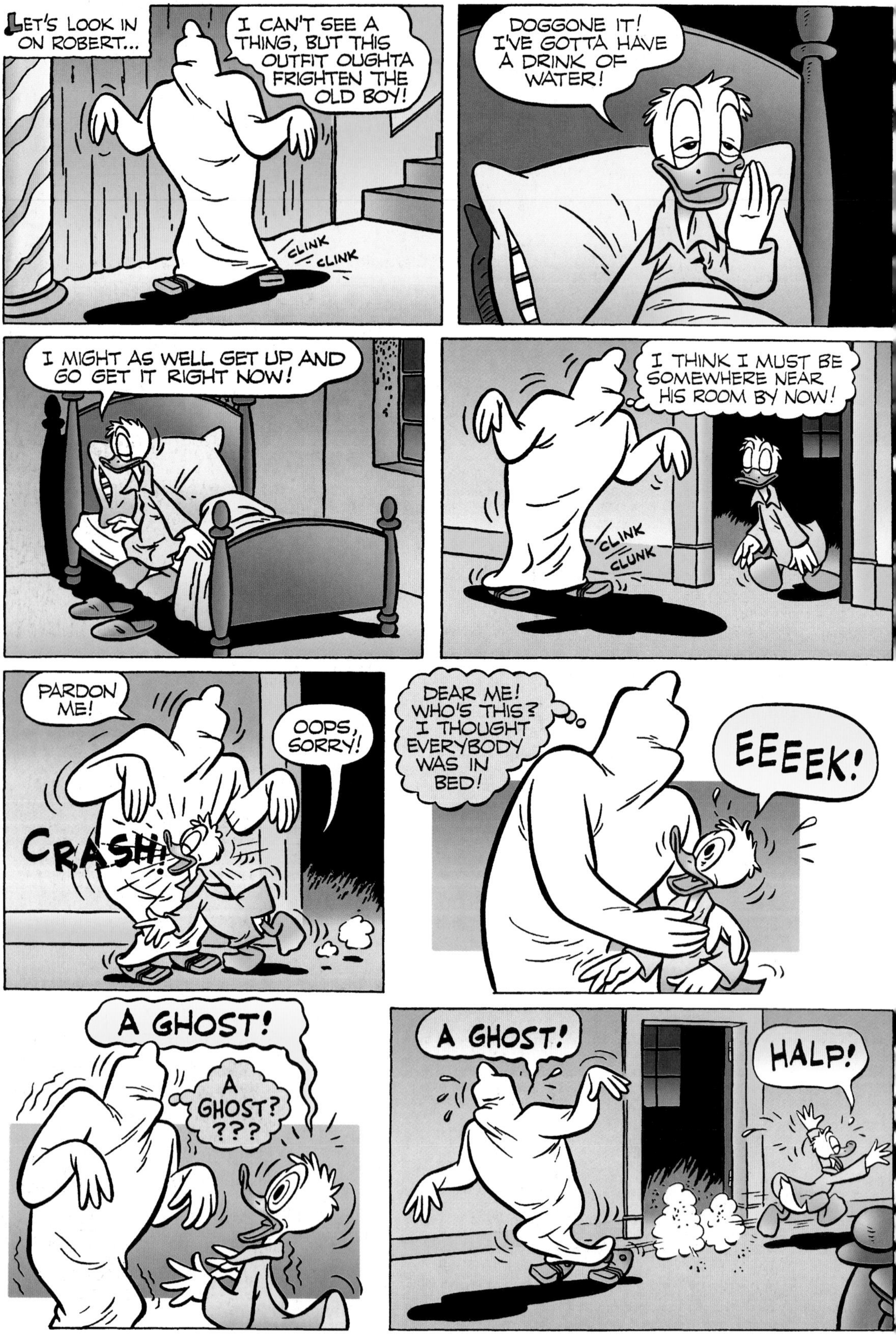
LET'S LOOK IN ON ROBERT...
I CAN'T SEE A THING, BUT THIS OUTFIT OUGHTA FRIGHTEN THE OLD BOY!
CLINK
CLINK
DOGGONE IT! I'VE GOTTA HAVE A DRINK OF WATER!
I MIGHT AS WELL GET UP AND GO GET IT RIGHT NOW!
I THINK I MUST BE SOMEWHERE NEAR HIS ROOM BY NOW!
CLINK
CLUNK
PARDON ME!
OOPS, SORRY!
CRASH!
DEAR ME! WHO'S THIS? I THOUGHT EVERYBODY WAS IN BED!
EEEEK!
A GHOST!
A GHOST? ???
A GHOST!
HALP!

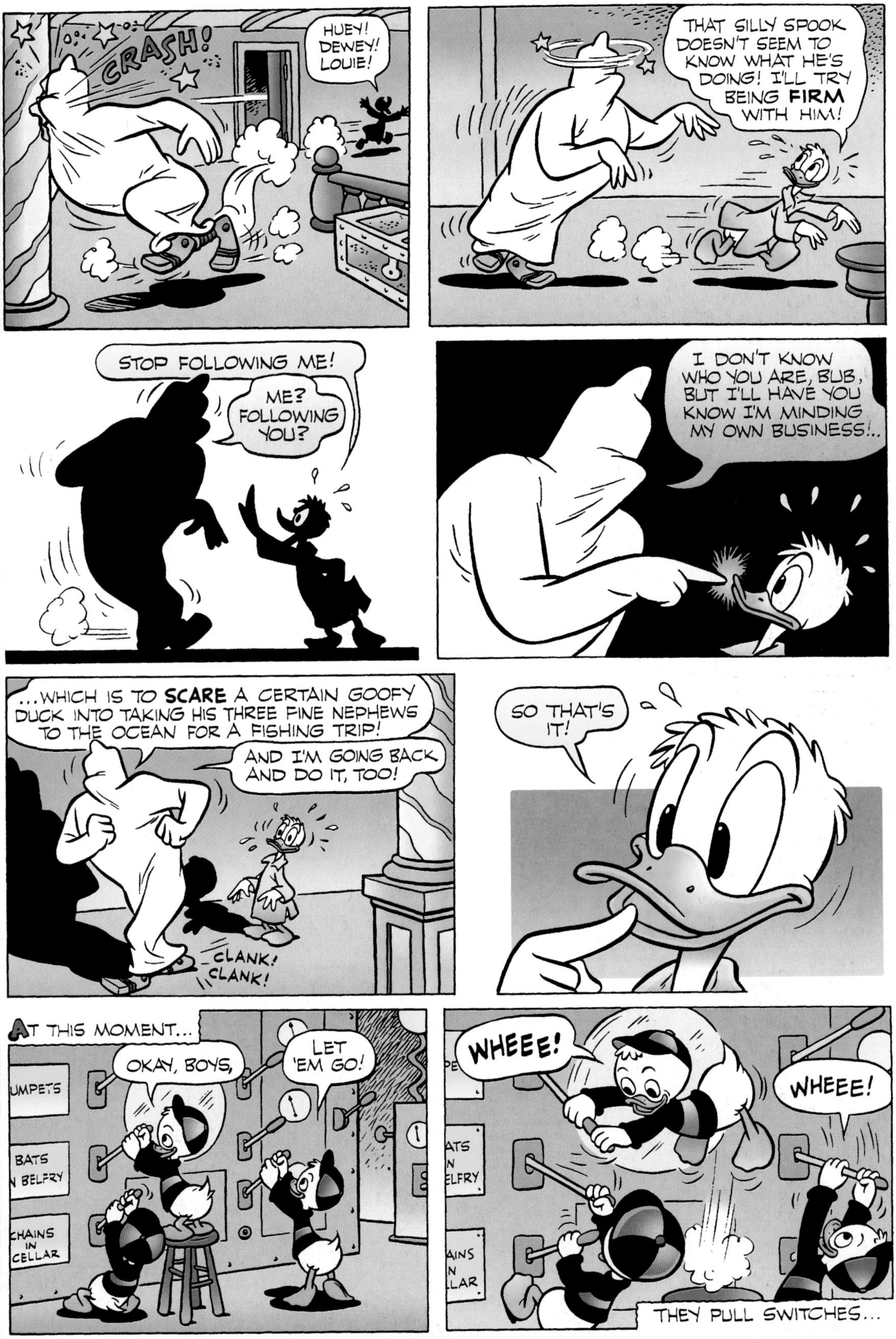
CRASH!
HUEY! DEWEY! LOUIE!
THAT SILLY SPOOK DOESN'T SEEM TO KNOW WHAT HE'S DOING! I'LL TRY BEING FIRM WITH HIM!
STOP FOLLOWING ME!
ME? FOLLOWING YOU?
I DON'T KNOW WHO YOU ARE, BUB, BUT I'LL HAVE YOU KNOW I'M MINDING MY OWN BUSINESS!..
...WHICH IS TO SCARE A CERTAIN GOOFY DUCK INTO TAKING HIS THREE FINE NEPHEWS TO THE OCEAN FOR A FISHING TRIP!
AND I'M GOING BACK AND DO IT, TOO!
CLANK! CLANK!
SO THAT'S IT!
AT THIS MOMENT...
OKAY, BOYS,
LET 'EM GO!
UMPETS
BATS N BELFRY
CHAINS IN CELLAR
WHEEE!
WHEEE!
THEY PULL SWITCHES...

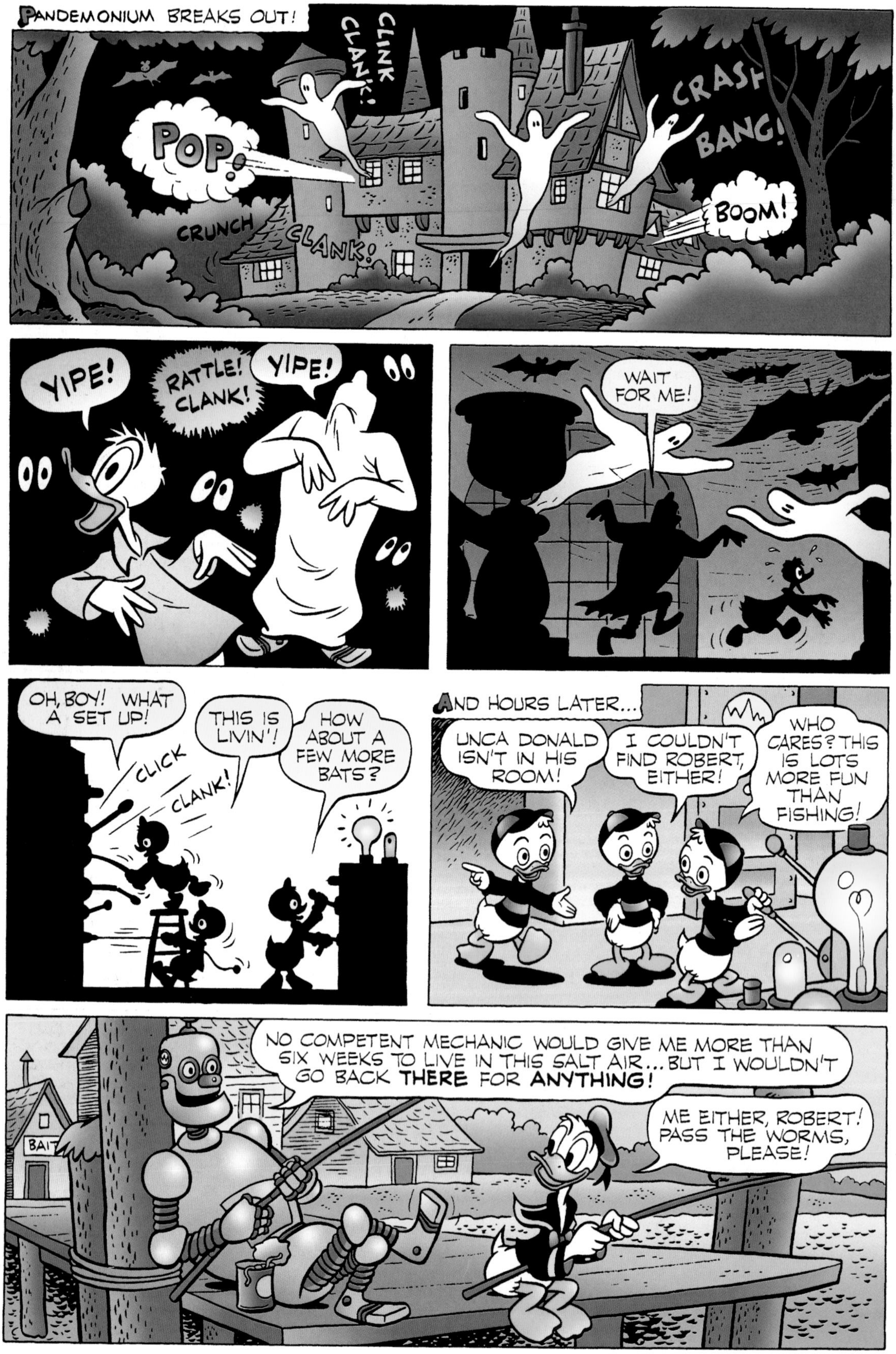
PANDEMONIUM BREAKS OUT!
CLINK CLANK!
POP!
CRASH
BANG!
CRUNCH
CLANK!
BOOM!
YIPE!
RATTLE! CLANK!
YIPE!
WAIT FOR ME!
OH, BOY! WHAT A SET UP!
CLICK
CLANK!
THIS IS LIVIN'!
HOW ABOUT A FEW MORE BATS?
AND HOURS LATER...
UNCA DONALD ISN'T IN HIS ROOM!
I COULDN'T FIND ROBERT, EITHER!
WHO CARES? THIS IS LOTS MORE FUN THAN FISHING!
NO COMPETENT MECHANIC WOULD GIVE ME MORE THAN SIX WEEKS TO LIVE IN THIS SALT AIR... BUT I WOULDN'T GO BACK THERE FOR ANYTHING!
ME EITHER, ROBERT! PASS THE WORMS, PLEASE!
BAIT

Walt Disney's SCAMP in Just Like Pop

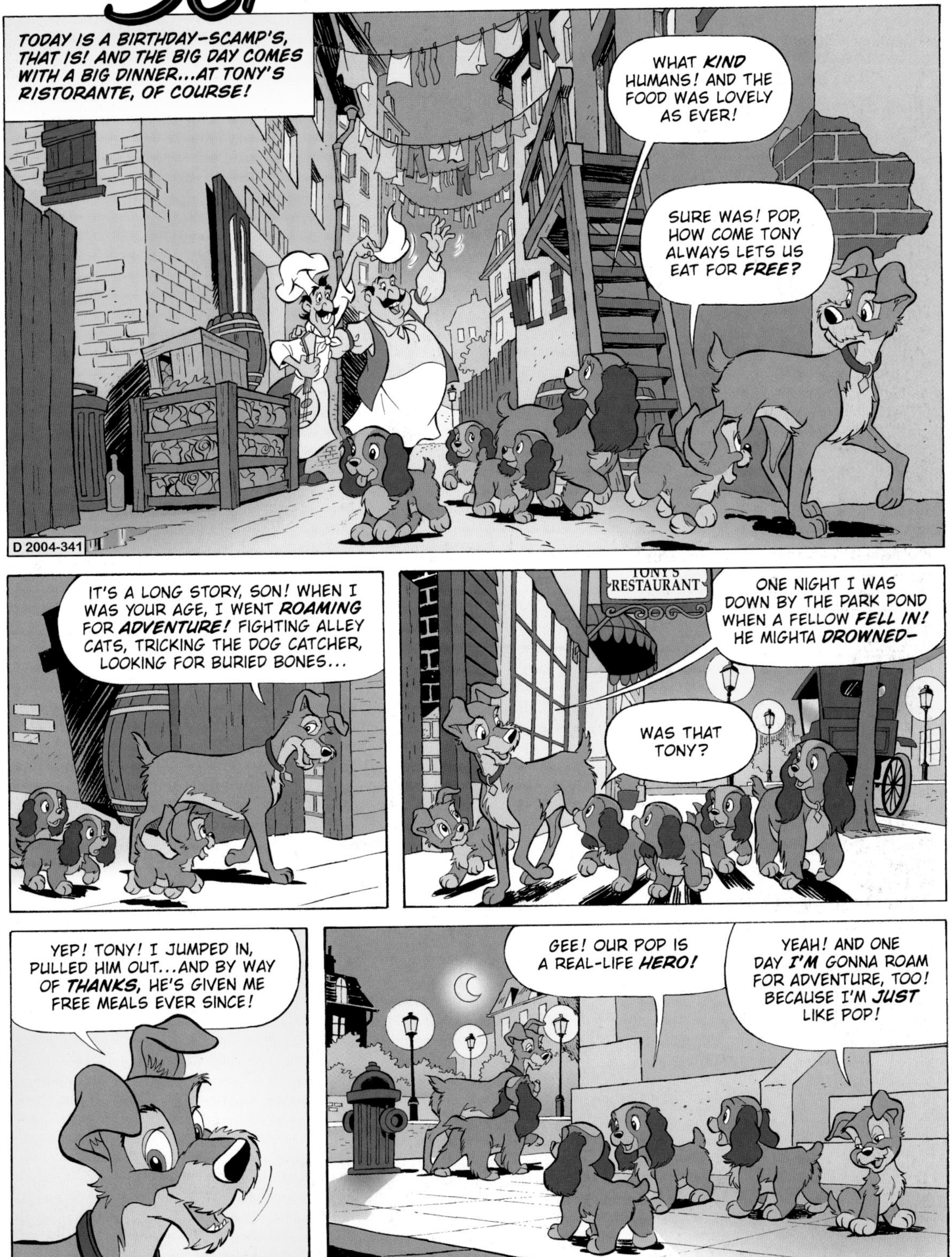
TODAY IS A BIRTHDAY—SCAMP'S, THAT IS! AND THE BIG DAY COMES WITH A BIG DINNER...AT TONY'S RISTORANTE, OF COURSE!
WHAT KIND HUMANS! AND THE FOOD WAS LOVELY AS EVER!
SURE WAS! POP, HOW COME TONY ALWAYS LETS US EAT FOR FREE?
D 2004-341
IT'S A LONG STORY, SON! WHEN I WAS YOUR AGE, I WENT ROAMING FOR ADVENTURE! FIGHTING ALLEY CATS, TRICKING THE DOG CATCHER, LOOKING FOR BURIED BONES...
TONY'S RESTAURANT
ONE NIGHT I WAS DOWN BY THE PARK POND WHEN A FELLOW FELL IN! HE MIGHTA DROWNED—
WAS THAT TONY?
YEP! TONY! I JUMPED IN, PULLED HIM OUT...AND BY WAY OF THANKS, HE'S GIVEN ME FREE MEALS EVER SINCE!
GEE! OUR POP IS A REAL-LIFE HERO!
YEAH! AND ONE DAY I'M GONNA ROAM FOR ADVENTURE, TOO! BECAUSE I'M JUST LIKE POP!

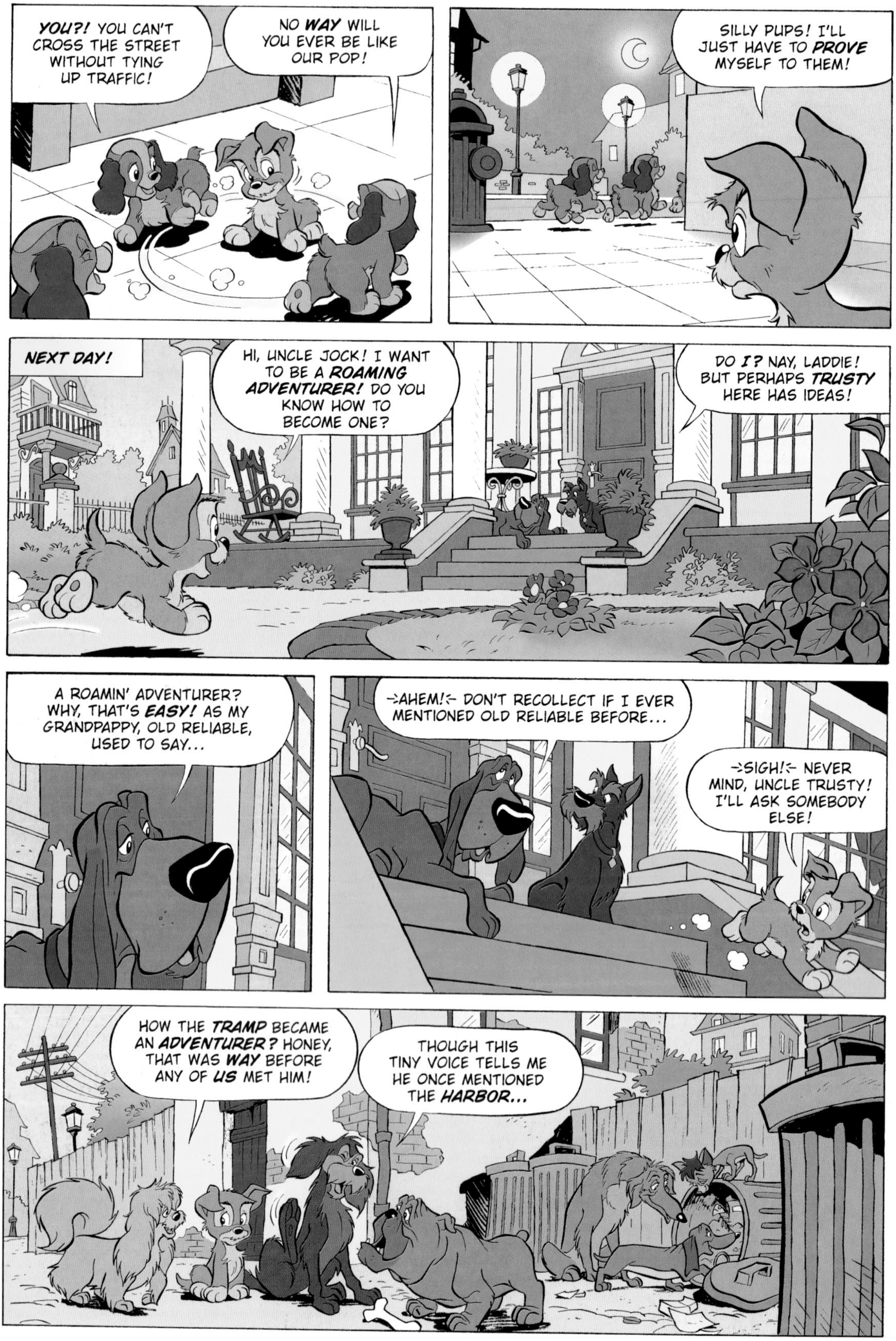
YOU?! YOU CAN'T CROSS THE STREET WITHOUT TYING UP TRAFFIC!
NO WAY WILL YOU EVER BE LIKE OUR POP!
SILLY PUPS! I'LL JUST HAVE TO PROVE MYSELF TO THEM!
NEXT DAY!
HI, UNCLE JOCK! I WANT TO BE A ROAMING ADVENTURER! DO YOU KNOW HOW TO BECOME ONE?
DO I? NAY, LADDIE! BUT PERHAPS TRUSTY HERE HAS IDEAS!
A ROAMIN' ADVENTURER? WHY, THAT'S EASY! AS MY GRANDPAPPY, OLD RELIABLE, USED TO SAY...
-AHEM!- DON'T RECOLLECT IF I EVER MENTIONED OLD RELIABLE BEFORE...
-SIGH!- NEVER MIND, UNCLE TRUSTY! I'LL ASK SOMEBODY ELSE!
HOW THE TRAMP BECAME AN ADVENTURER? HONEY, THAT WAS WAY BEFORE ANY OF US MET HIM!
THOUGH THIS TINY VOICE TELLS ME HE ONCE MENTIONED THE HARBOR...

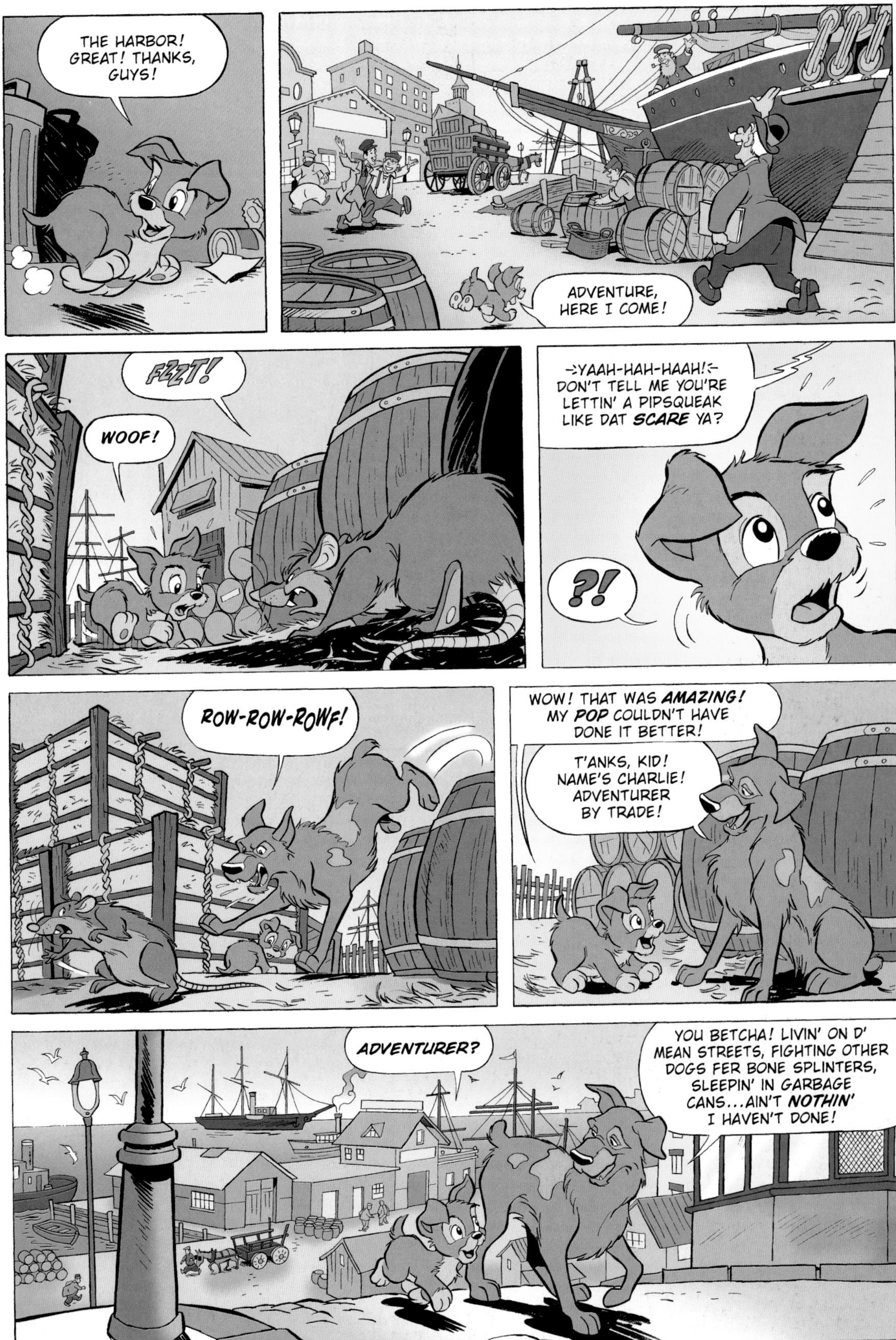
THE HARBOR! GREAT! THANKS, GUYS!
ADVENTURE, HERE I COME!
WOOF!
FZZT!
-YAAH-HAH-HAAH!- DON'T TELL ME YOU'RE LETTIN' A PIPSQUEAK LIKE DAT SCARE YA?
?!
ROW-ROW-ROWF!
WOW! THAT WAS AMAZING! MY POP COULDN'T HAVE DONE IT BETTER!
T'ANKS, KID! NAME'S CHARLIE! ADVENTURER BY TRADE!
ADVENTURER?
YOU BETCHA! LIVIN' ON D' MEAN STREETS, FIGHTING OTHER DOGS FER BONE SPLINTERS, SLEEPIN' IN GARBAGE CANS...AIN'T NOTHIN' I HAVEN'T DONE!

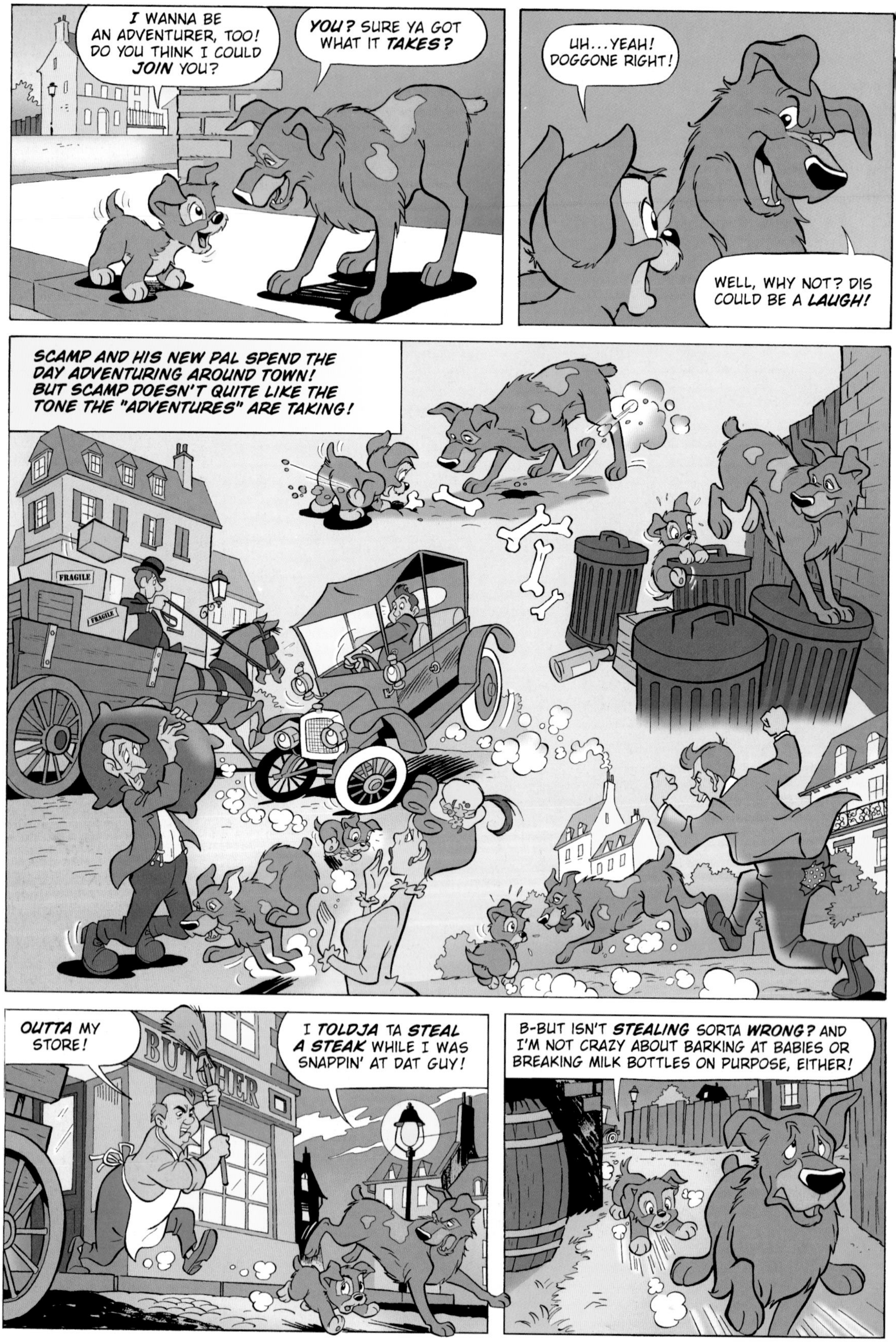
I WANNA BE AN ADVENTURER, TOO! DO YOU THINK I COULD JOIN YOU?
YOU? SURE YA GOT WHAT IT TAKES?
UH...YEAH! DOGGONE RIGHT!
WELL, WHY NOT? DIS COULD BE A LAUGH!
SCAMP AND HIS NEW PAL SPEND THE DAY ADVENTURING AROUND TOWN! BUT SCAMP DOESN'T QUITE LIKE THE TONE THE "ADVENTURES" ARE TAKING!
FRAGILE
FRAGILE
OUTTA MY STORE!
BUTCHER
I TOLDJA TA STEAL A STEAK WHILE I WAS SNAPPIN' AT DAT GUY!
B-BUT ISN'T STEALING SORTA WRONG? AND I'M NOT CRAZY ABOUT BARKING AT BABIES OR BREAKING MILK BOTTLES ON PURPOSE, EITHER!

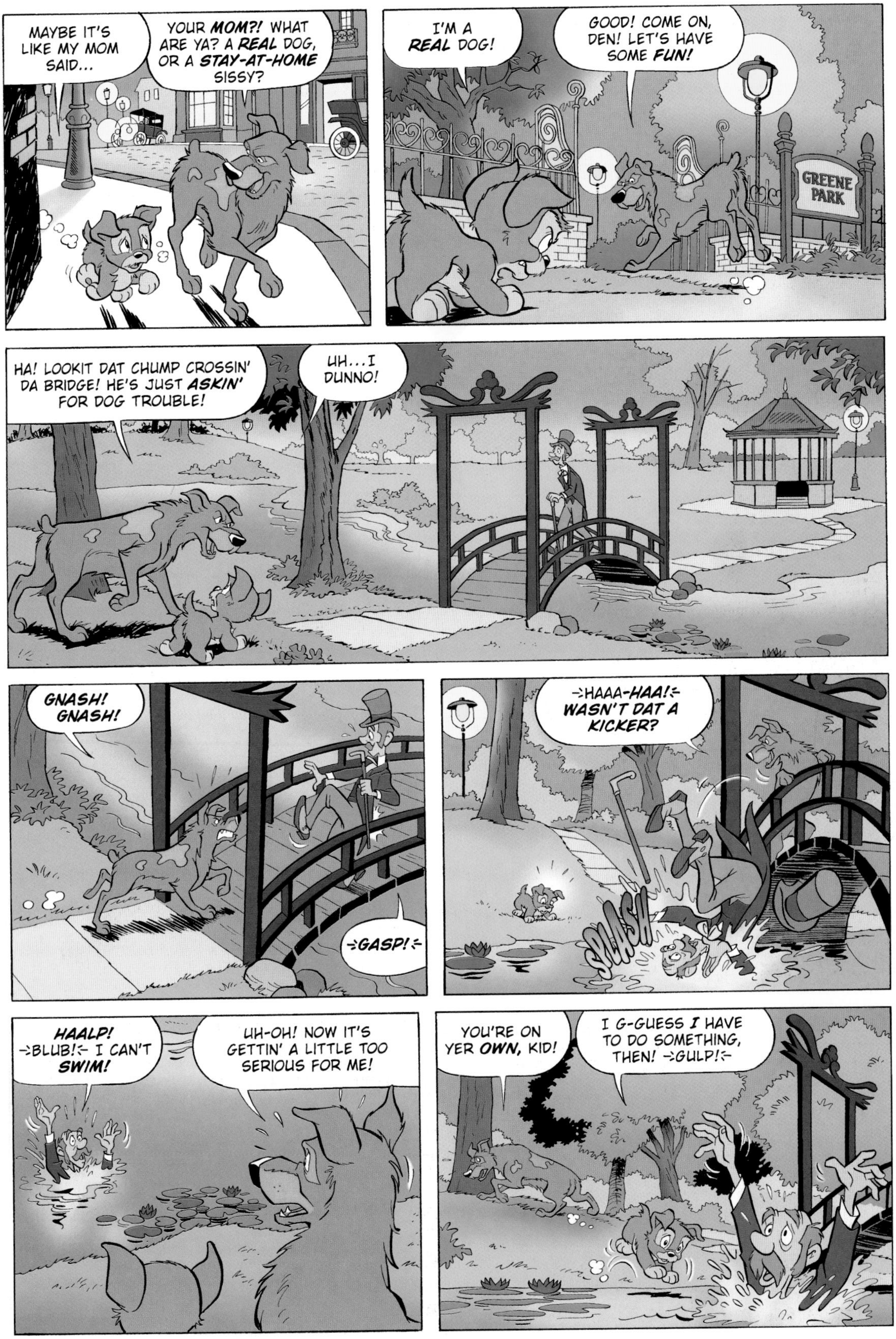
MAYBE IT'S LIKE MY MOM SAID...
YOUR MOM?! WHAT ARE YA? A REAL DOG, OR A STAY-AT-HOME SISSY?
I'M A REAL DOG!
GOOD! COME ON, DEN! LET'S HAVE SOME FUN!
GREENE PARK
HA! LOOKIT DAT CHUMP CROSSIN' DA BRIDGE! HE'S JUST ASKIN' FOR DOG TROUBLE!
UH...I DUNNO!
GNASH! GNASH!
GASP!
HAAA-HAA! WASN'T DAT A KICKER?
SPLASH
HAALP! BLUB! I CAN'T SWIM!
UH-OH! NOW IT'S GETTIN' A LITTLE TOO SERIOUS FOR ME!
YOU'RE ON YER OWN, KID!
I G-GUESS I HAVE TO DO SOMETHING, THEN! GULP!

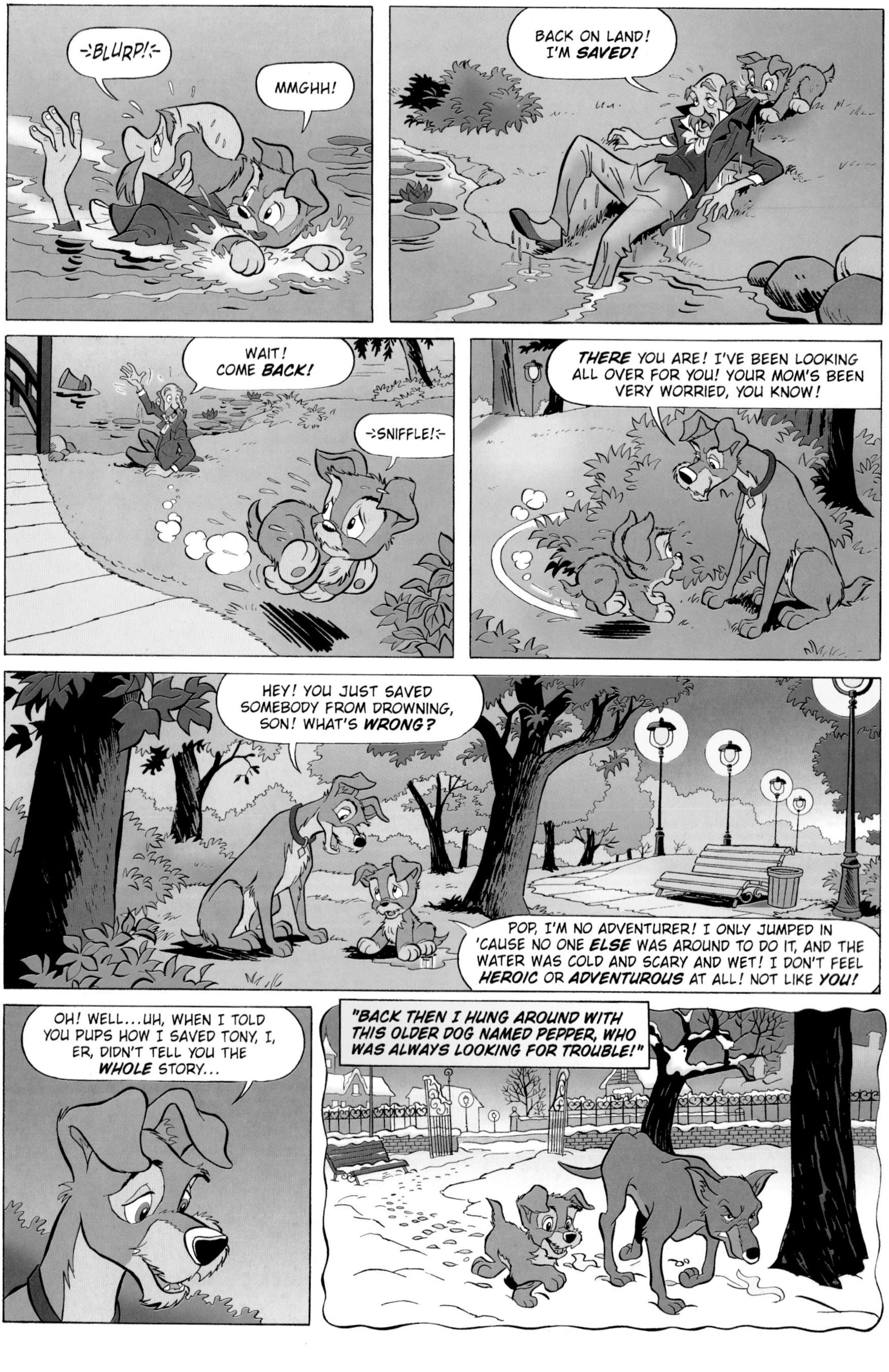

-BLURP!-
MMGHH!
BACK ON LAND! I'M *SAVED!*
WAIT! COME *BACK!*
-SNIFFLE!-
THERE YOU ARE! I'VE BEEN LOOKING ALL OVER FOR YOU! YOUR MOM'S BEEN VERY WORRIED, YOU KNOW!
HEY! YOU JUST SAVED SOMEBODY FROM DROWNING, SON! WHAT'S *WRONG?*
POP, I'M NO ADVENTURER! I ONLY JUMPED IN 'CAUSE NO ONE *ELSE* WAS AROUND TO DO IT, AND THE WATER WAS COLD AND SCARY AND WET! I DON'T FEEL *HEROIC* OR *ADVENTUROUS* AT ALL! NOT LIKE *YOU!*
OH! WELL...UH, WHEN I TOLD YOU PUPS HOW I SAVED TONY, I, ER, DIDN'T TELL YOU THE *WHOLE* STORY...
"BACK THEN I HUNG AROUND WITH THIS OLDER DOG NAMED PEPPER, WHO WAS ALWAYS LOOKING FOR TROUBLE!"

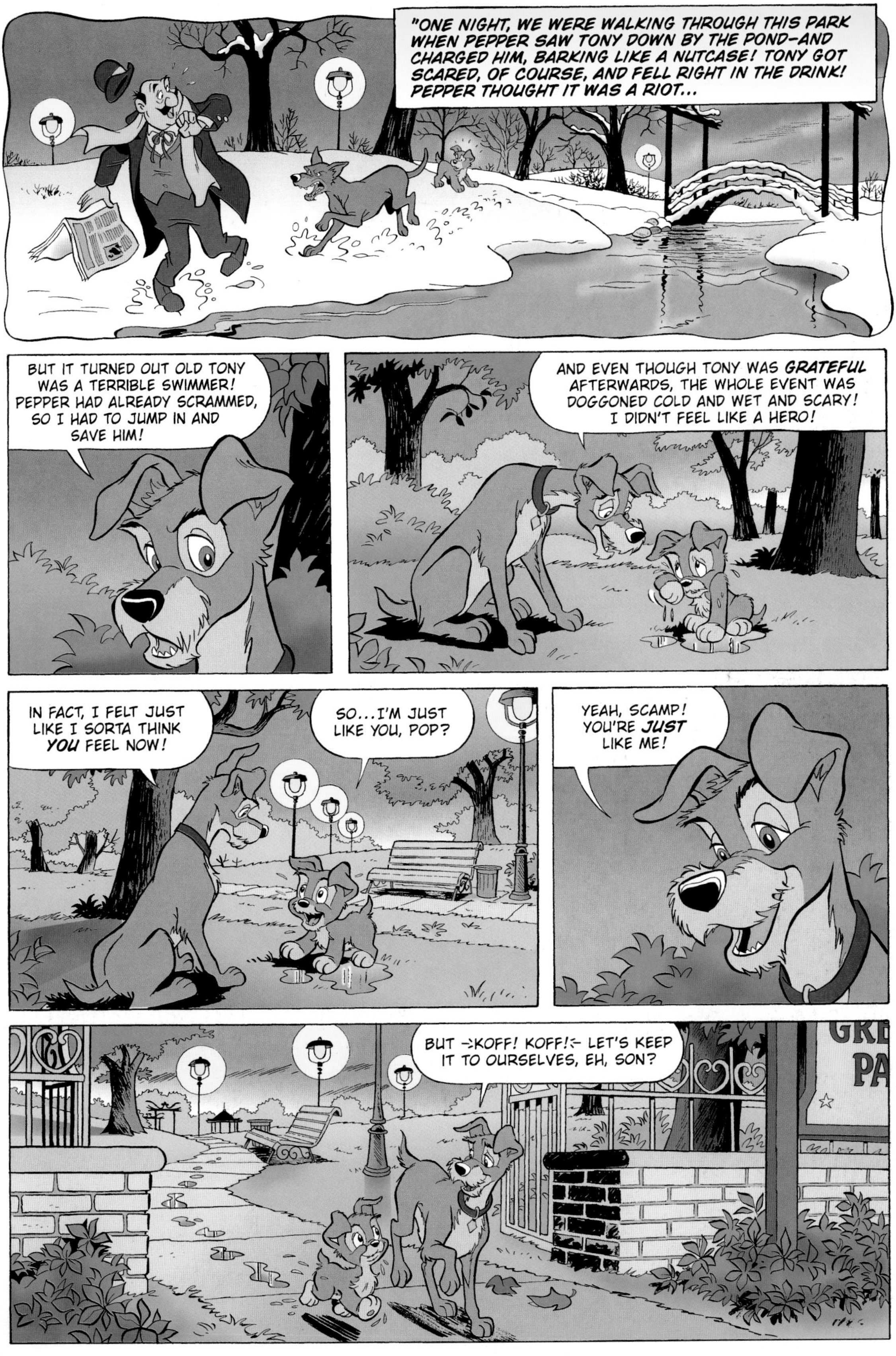
"ONE NIGHT, WE WERE WALKING THROUGH THIS PARK WHEN PEPPER SAW TONY DOWN BY THE POND—AND CHARGED HIM, BARKING LIKE A NUTCASE! TONY GOT SCARED, OF COURSE, AND FELL RIGHT IN THE DRINK! PEPPER THOUGHT IT WAS A RIOT...
BUT IT TURNED OUT OLD TONY WAS A TERRIBLE SWIMMER! PEPPER HAD ALREADY SCRAMMED, SO I HAD TO JUMP IN AND SAVE HIM!
AND EVEN THOUGH TONY WAS GRATEFUL AFTERWARDS, THE WHOLE EVENT WAS DOGGONED COLD AND WET AND SCARY! I DIDN'T FEEL LIKE A HERO!
IN FACT, I FELT JUST LIKE I SORTA THINK YOU FEEL NOW!
SO...I'M JUST LIKE YOU, POP?
YEAH, SCAMP! YOU'RE JUST LIKE ME!
BUT ⇾KOFF! KOFF!⇽ LET'S KEEP IT TO OURSELVES, EH, SON?

© 2006 Disney
Enterprises Inc.

Delivered right to your door!

We know how much you enjoy visiting your local comic shop, but wouldn't it be nice to have your favorite Disney comics delivered to you? Subscribe today and we'll send the latest issues of your favorite comics directly to your doorstep. And if you would still prefer to browse through the latest in comic art but aren't sure where to go, check out the Comic Shop Locator Service at www.diamondcomics.com/csls or call 1-888-COMIC-BOOK.

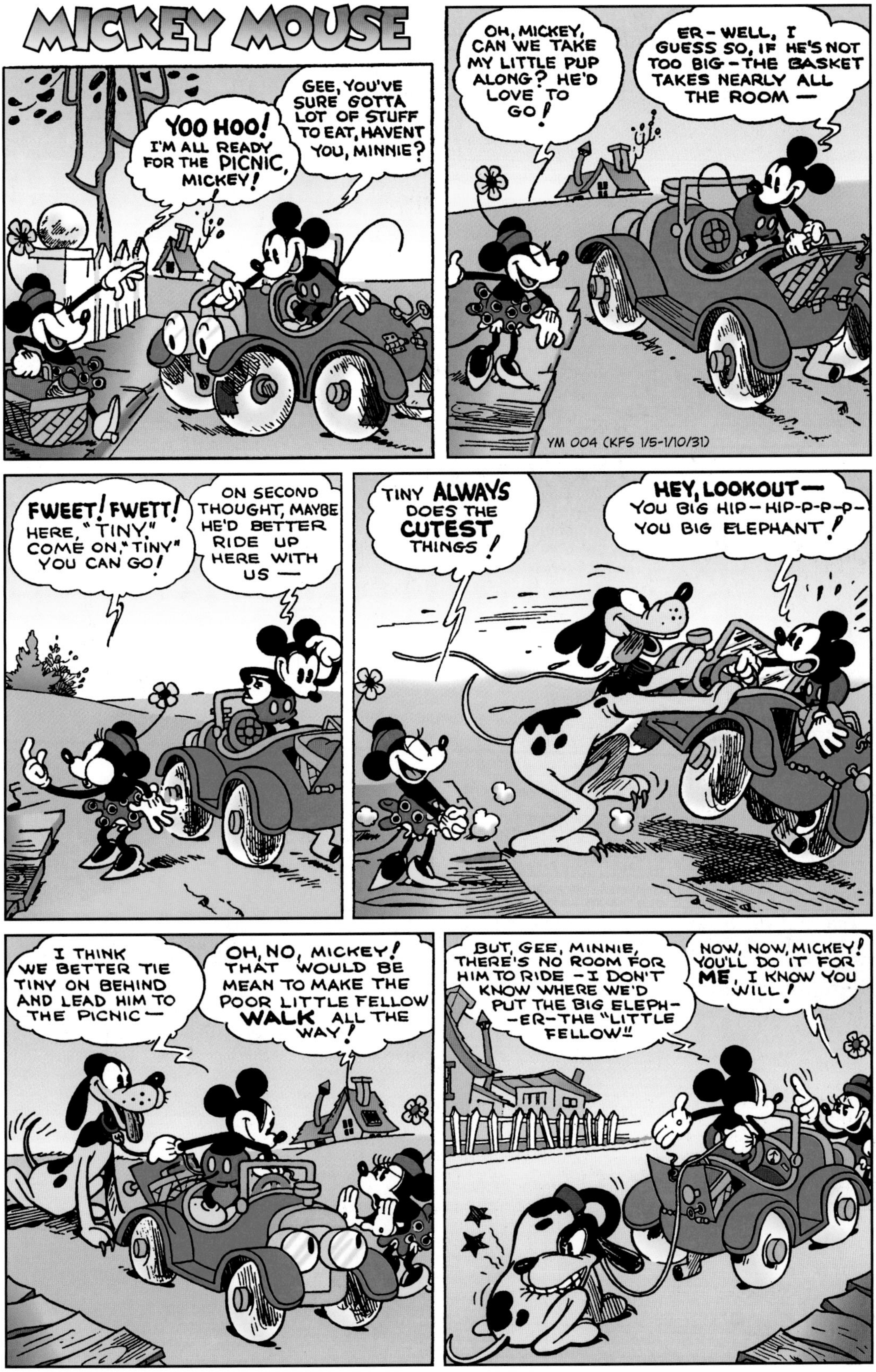
MICKEY MOUSE
YOO HOO! I'M ALL READY FOR THE PICNIC, MICKEY!
GEE, YOU'VE SURE GOTTA LOT OF STUFF TO EAT, HAVENT YOU, MINNIE?
OH, MICKEY, CAN WE TAKE MY LITTLE PUP ALONG? HE'D LOVE TO GO!
ER - WELL, I GUESS SO, IF HE'S NOT TOO BIG - THE BASKET TAKES NEARLY ALL THE ROOM —
YM 004 (KFS 1/5-1/10/31)
FWEET! FWETT! HERE, "TINY." COME ON, "TINY" YOU CAN GO!
ON SECOND THOUGHT, MAYBE HE'D BETTER RIDE UP HERE WITH US —
TINY ALWAYS DOES THE CUTEST THINGS!
HEY, LOOKOUT — YOU BIG HIP - HIP-P-P-P- YOU BIG ELEPHANT!
I THINK WE BETTER TIE TINY ON BEHIND AND LEAD HIM TO THE PICNIC —
OH, NO, MICKEY! THAT WOULD BE MEAN TO MAKE THE POOR LITTLE FELLOW WALK ALL THE WAY!
BUT, GEE, MINNIE, THERE'S NO ROOM FOR HIM TO RIDE - I DON'T KNOW WHERE WE'D PUT THE BIG ELEPH- -ER-THE "LITTLE FELLOW!"
NOW, NOW, MICKEY! YOU'LL DO IT FOR ME, I KNOW YOU WILL!

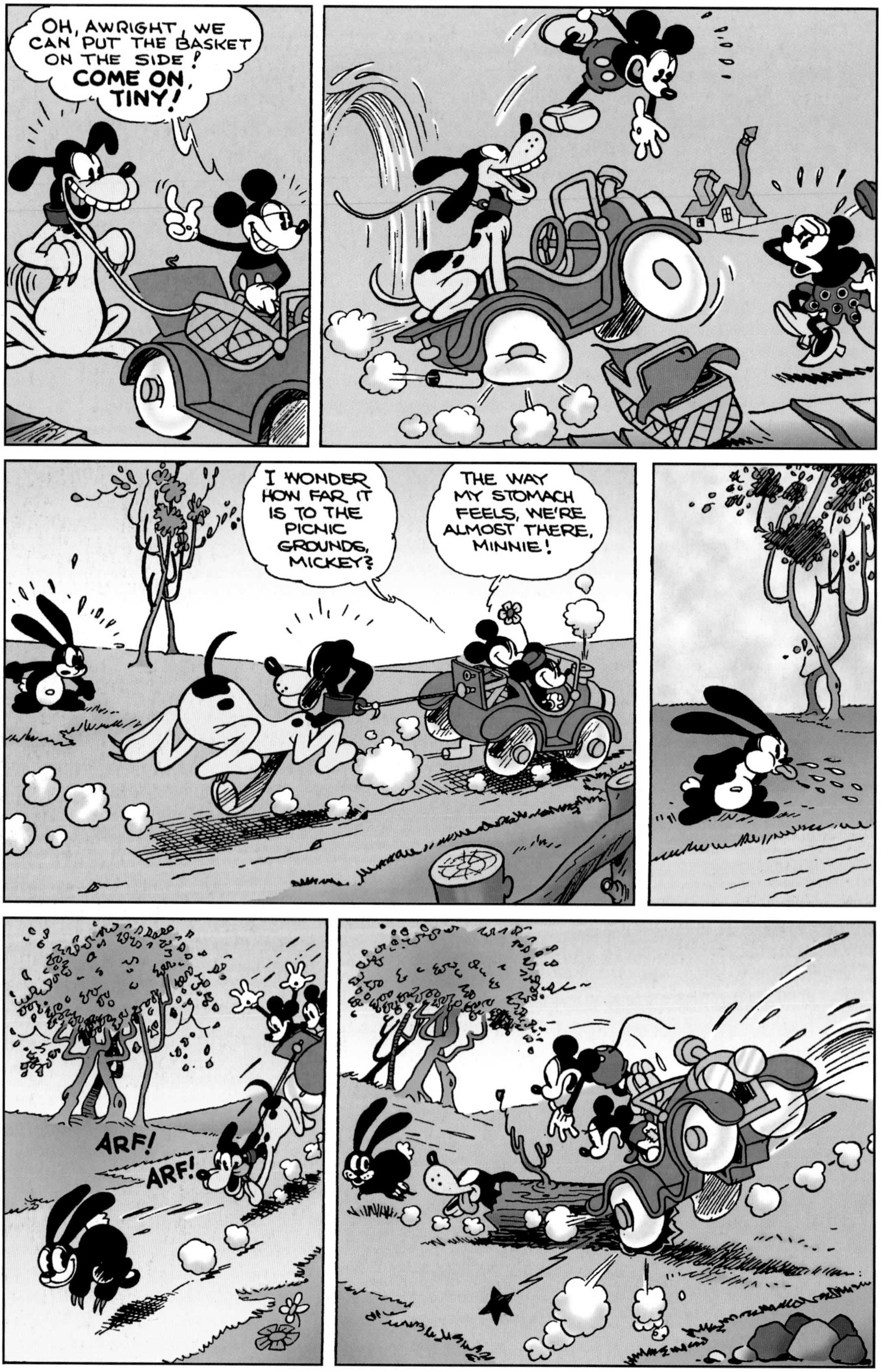
OH, AWRIGHT, WE CAN PUT THE BASKET ON THE SIDE! COME ON, TINY!
I WONDER HOW FAR IT IS TO THE PICNIC GROUNDS, MICKEY?
THE WAY MY STOMACH FEELS, WE'RE ALMOST THERE, MINNIE!
ARF!
ARF!

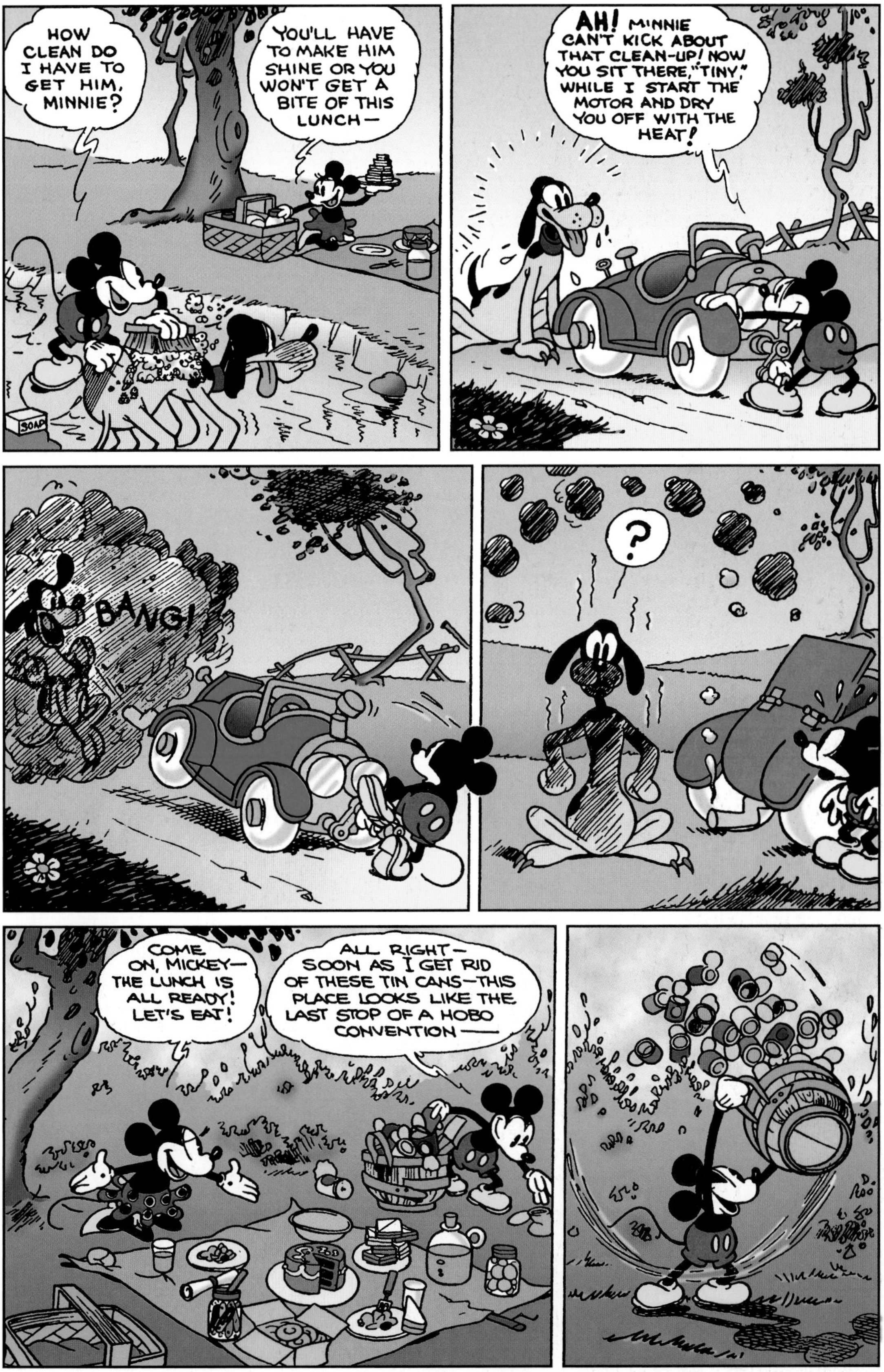
HOW CLEAN DO I HAVE TO GET HIM, MINNIE?
YOU'LL HAVE TO MAKE HIM SHINE OR YOU WON'T GET A BITE OF THIS LUNCH—
SOAP
AH! MINNIE CAN'T KICK ABOUT THAT CLEAN-UP! NOW YOU SIT THERE, "TINY," WHILE I START THE MOTOR AND DRY YOU OFF WITH THE HEAT!
BANG!
?
COME ON, MICKEY— THE LUNCH IS ALL READY! LET'S EAT!
ALL RIGHT— SOON AS I GET RID OF THESE TIN CANS—THIS PLACE LOOKS LIKE THE LAST STOP OF A HOBO CONVENTION——

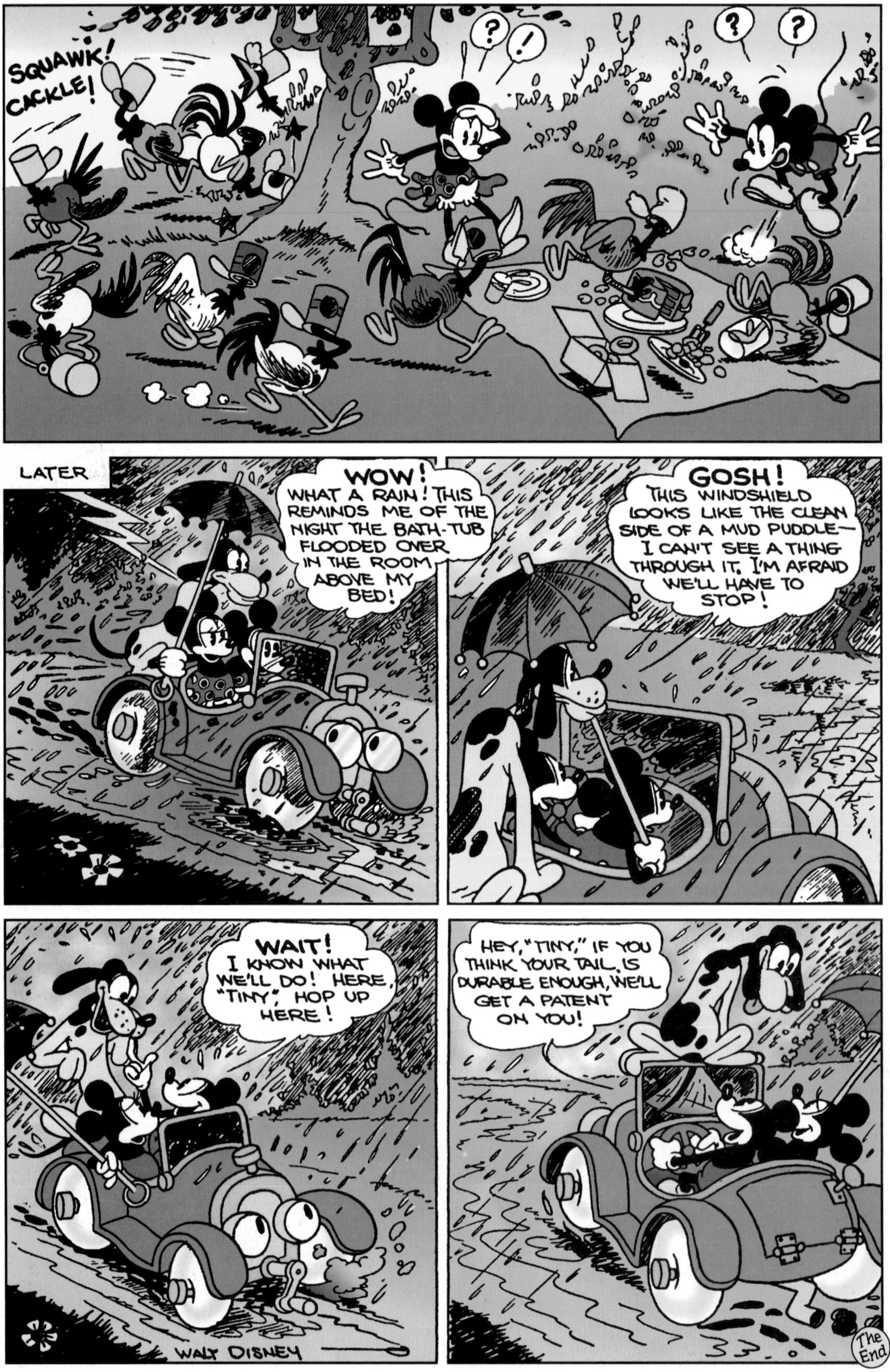
SQUAWK!
CACKLE!
?
!
?
?
LATER
WOW! WHAT A RAIN! THIS REMINDS ME OF THE NIGHT THE BATH-TUB FLOODED OVER IN THE ROOM ABOVE MY BED!
GOSH! THIS WINDSHIELD LOOKS LIKE THE CLEAN SIDE OF A MUD PUDDLE— I CAN'T SEE A THING THROUGH IT. I'M AFRAID WE'LL HAVE TO STOP!
WAIT! I KNOW WHAT WE'LL DO! HERE, "TINY," HOP UP HERE!
WALT DISNEY
HEY, "TINY," IF YOU THINK YOUR TAIL IS DURABLE ENOUGH, WE'LL GET A PATENT ON YOU!
The End

Walt Disney's Donald Duck

THE MAGNIFICENT SEVEN (minus 4) CABALLEROS

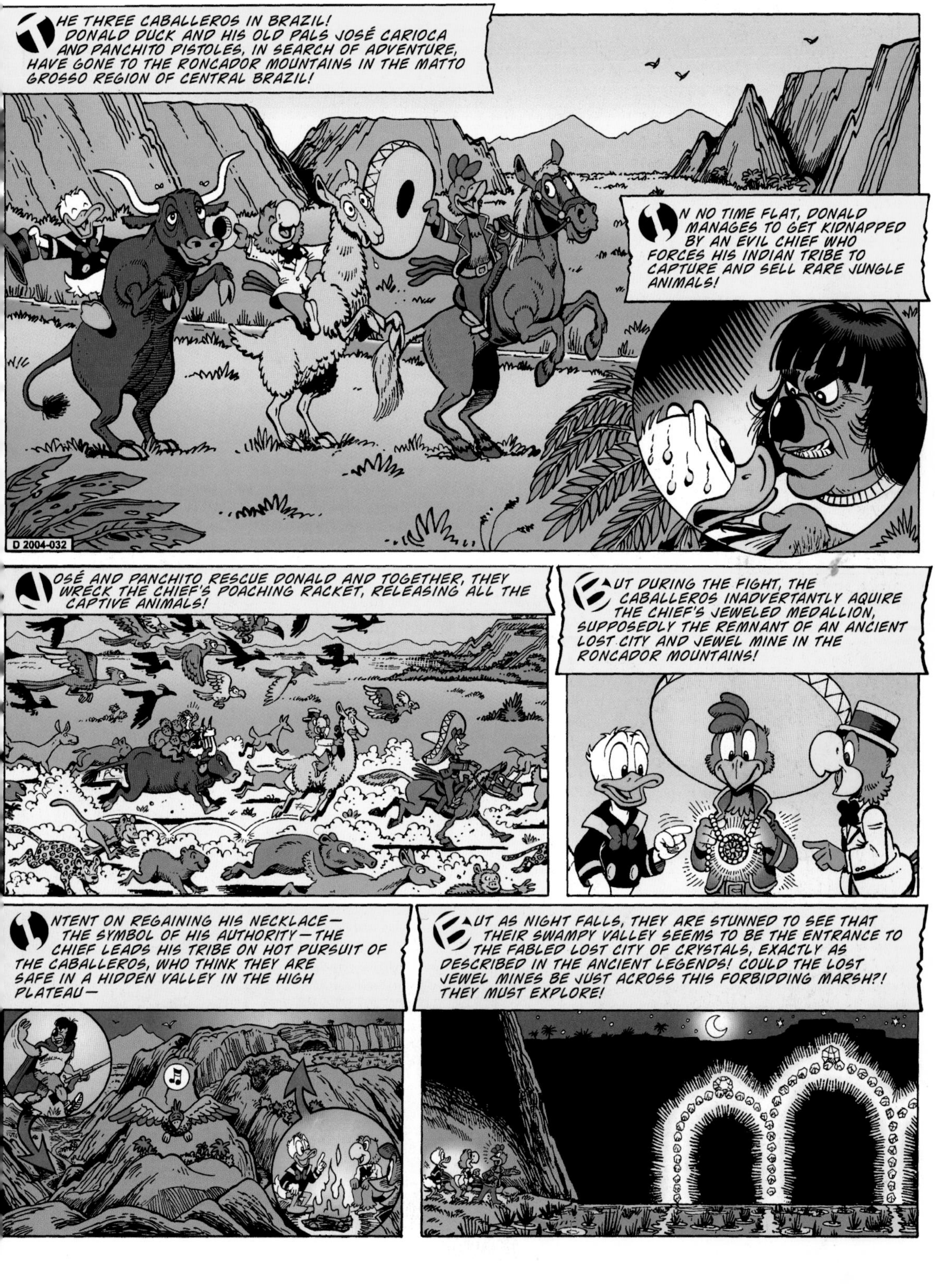
THE THREE CABALLEROS IN BRAZIL! DONALD DUCK AND HIS OLD PALS JOSÉ CARIOCA AND PANCHITO PISTOLES, IN SEARCH OF ADVENTURE, HAVE GONE TO THE RONCADOR MOUNTAINS IN THE MATTO GROSSO REGION OF CENTRAL BRAZIL!
IN NO TIME FLAT, DONALD MANAGES TO GET KIDNAPPED BY AN EVIL CHIEF WHO FORCES HIS INDIAN TRIBE TO CAPTURE AND SELL RARE JUNGLE ANIMALS!
D 2004-032
JOSÉ AND PANCHITO RESCUE DONALD AND TOGETHER, THEY WRECK THE CHIEF'S POACHING RACKET, RELEASING ALL THE CAPTIVE ANIMALS!
BUT DURING THE FIGHT, THE CABALLEROS INADVERTANTLY AQUIRE THE CHIEF'S JEWELED MEDALLION, SUPPOSEDLY THE REMNANT OF AN ANCIENT LOST CITY AND JEWEL MINE IN THE RONCADOR MOUNTAINS!
INTENT ON REGAINING HIS NECKLACE— THE SYMBOL OF HIS AUTHORITY—THE CHIEF LEADS HIS TRIBE ON HOT PURSUIT OF THE CABALLEROS, WHO THINK THEY ARE SAFE IN A HIDDEN VALLEY IN THE HIGH PLATEAU—
BUT AS NIGHT FALLS, THEY ARE STUNNED TO SEE THAT THEIR SWAMPY VALLEY SEEMS TO BE THE ENTRANCE TO THE FABLED LOST CITY OF CRYSTALS, EXACTLY AS DESCRIBED IN THE ANCIENT LEGENDS! COULD THE LOST JEWEL MINES BE JUST ACROSS THIS FORBIDDING MARSH?! THEY MUST EXPLORE!

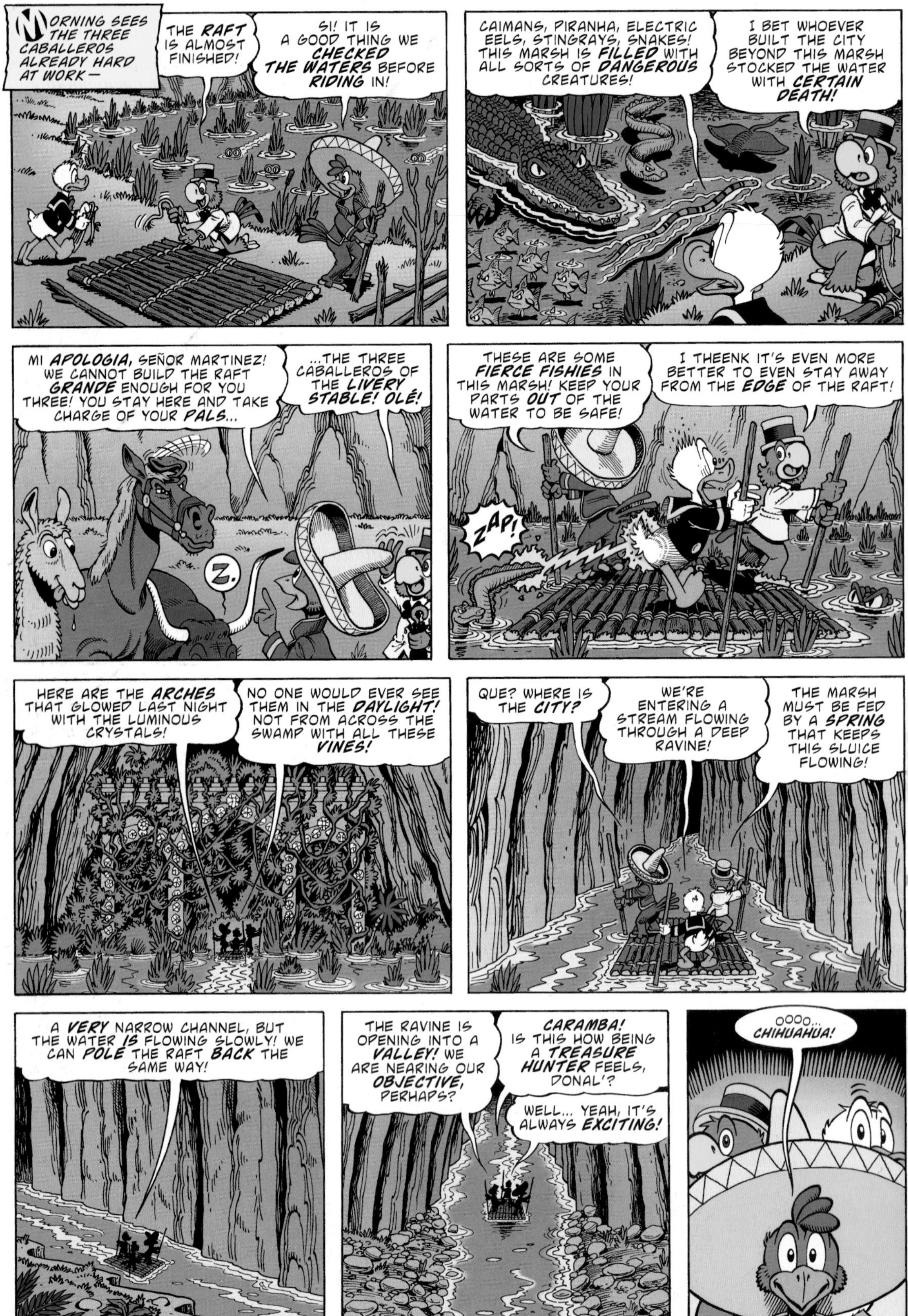
MORNING SEES THE THREE CABALLEROS ALREADY HARD AT WORK—
THE RAFT IS ALMOST FINISHED!
SI! IT IS A GOOD THING WE CHECKED THE WATERS BEFORE RIDING IN!
CAIMANS, PIRANHA, ELECTRIC EELS, STINGRAYS, SNAKES! THIS MARSH IS FILLED WITH ALL SORTS OF DANGEROUS CREATURES!
I BET WHOEVER BUILT THE CITY BEYOND THIS MARSH STOCKED THE WATER WITH CERTAIN DEATH!
MI APOLOGIA, SEÑOR MARTINEZ! WE CANNOT BUILD THE RAFT GRANDE ENOUGH FOR YOU THREE! YOU STAY HERE AND TAKE CHARGE OF YOUR PALS...
...THE THREE CABALLEROS OF THE LIVERY STABLE! OLÉ!
Z.
THESE ARE SOME FIERCE FISHIES IN THIS MARSH! KEEP YOUR PARTS OUT OF THE WATER TO BE SAFE!
I THEENK IT'S EVEN MORE BETTER TO EVEN STAY AWAY FROM THE EDGE OF THE RAFT!
ZAP!
HERE ARE THE ARCHES THAT GLOWED LAST NIGHT WITH THE LUMINOUS CRYSTALS!
NO ONE WOULD EVER SEE THEM IN THE DAYLIGHT! NOT FROM ACROSS THE SWAMP WITH ALL THESE VINES!
QUE? WHERE IS THE CITY?
WE'RE ENTERING A STREAM FLOWING THROUGH A DEEP RAVINE!
THE MARSH MUST BE FED BY A SPRING THAT KEEPS THIS SLUICE FLOWING!
A VERY NARROW CHANNEL, BUT THE WATER IS FLOWING SLOWLY! WE CAN POLE THE RAFT BACK THE SAME WAY!
THE RAVINE IS OPENING INTO A VALLEY! WE ARE NEARING OUR OBJECTIVE, PERHAPS?
CARAMBA! IS THIS HOW BEING A TREASURE HUNTER FEELS, DONAL'?
WELL... YEAH, IT'S ALWAYS EXCITING!
OOOO... CHIHUAHUA!

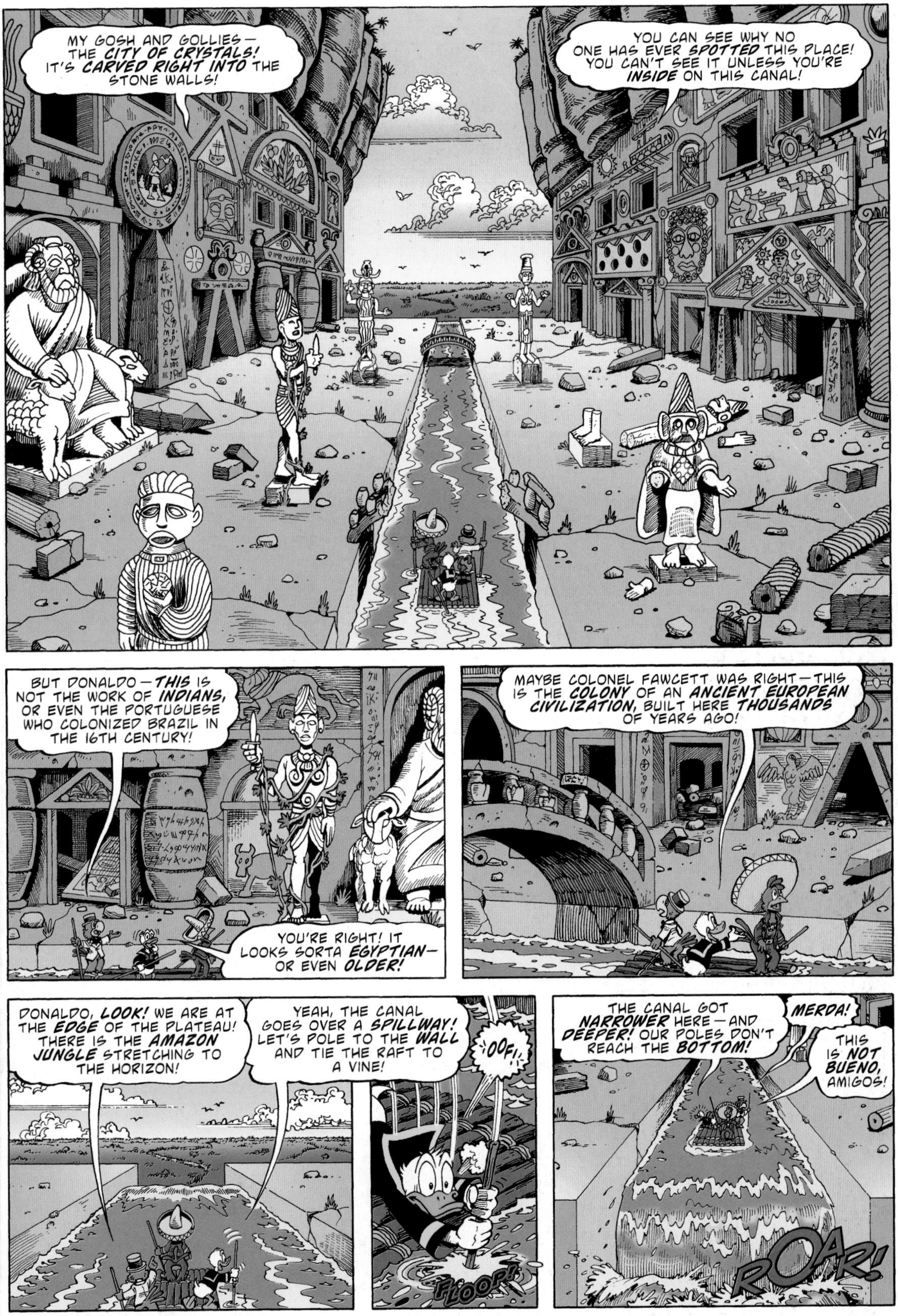
MY GOSH AND GOLLIES— THE CITY OF CRYSTALS! IT'S CARVED RIGHT INTO THE STONE WALLS!
YOU CAN SEE WHY NO ONE HAS EVER SPOTTED THIS PLACE! YOU CAN'T SEE IT UNLESS YOU'RE INSIDE ON THIS CANAL!
BUT DONALDO—THIS IS NOT THE WORK OF INDIANS, OR EVEN THE PORTUGUESE WHO COLONIZED BRAZIL IN THE 16TH CENTURY!
YOU'RE RIGHT! IT LOOKS SORTA EGYPTIAN— OR EVEN OLDER!
MAYBE COLONEL FAWCETT WAS RIGHT—THIS IS THE COLONY OF AN ANCIENT EUROPEAN CIVILIZATION, BUILT HERE THOUSANDS OF YEARS AGO!
DONALDO, LOOK! WE ARE AT THE EDGE OF THE PLATEAU! THERE IS THE AMAZON JUNGLE STRETCHING TO THE HORIZON!
YEAH, THE CANAL GOES OVER A SPILLWAY! LET'S POLE TO THE WALL AND TIE THE RAFT TO A VINE!
OOF!
FLOOP!
THE CANAL GOT NARROWER HERE—AND DEEPER! OUR POLES DON'T REACH THE BOTTOM!
MERDA!
THIS IS NOT BUENO, AMIGOS!
ROAR!

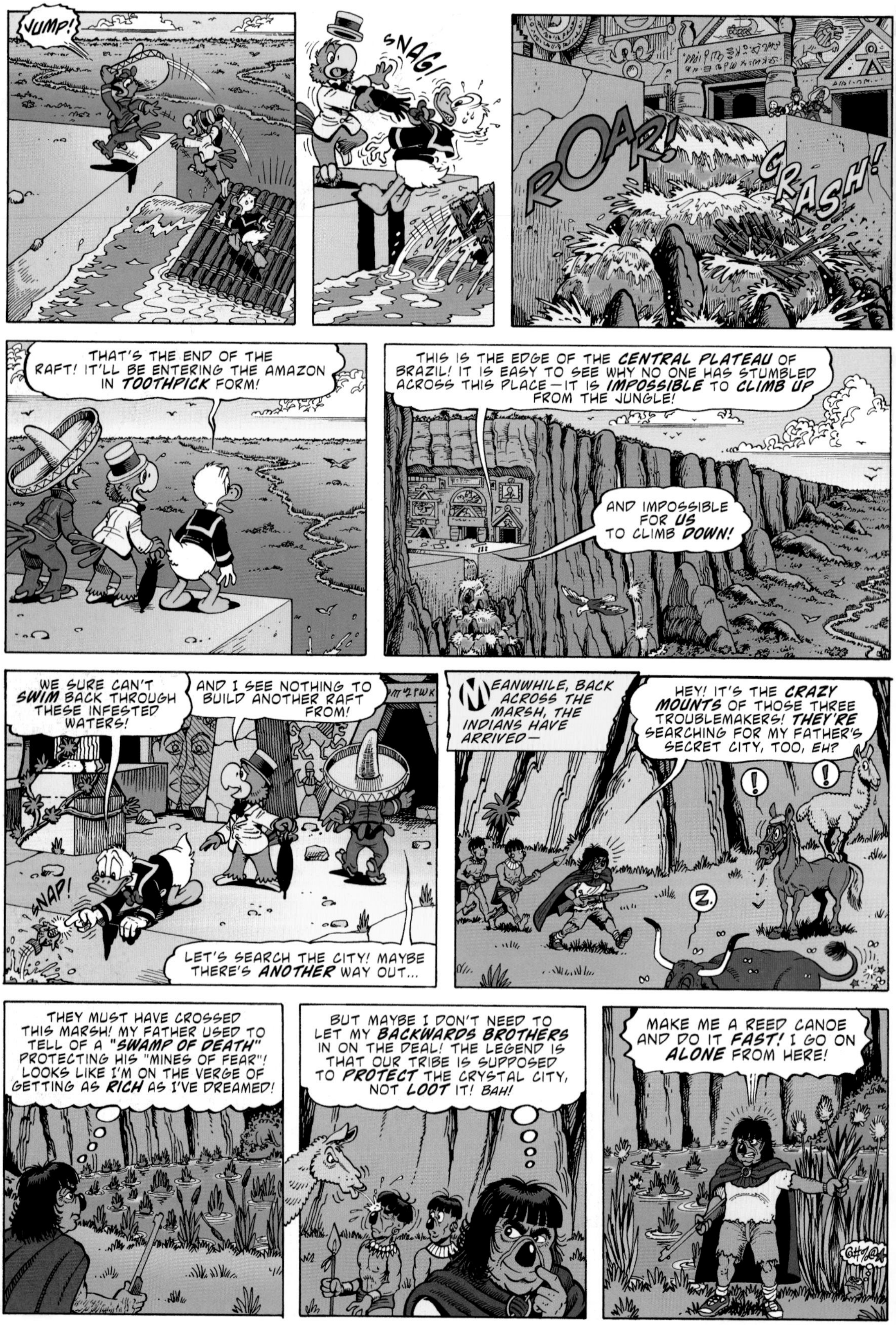
JUMP!
SNAG!
ROAR!
CRASH!
THAT'S THE END OF THE RAFT! IT'LL BE ENTERING THE AMAZON IN TOOTHPICK FORM!
THIS IS THE EDGE OF THE CENTRAL PLATEAU OF BRAZIL! IT IS EASY TO SEE WHY NO ONE HAS STUMBLED ACROSS THIS PLACE—IT IS IMPOSSIBLE TO CLIMB UP FROM THE JUNGLE!
AND IMPOSSIBLE FOR US TO CLIMB DOWN!
WE SURE CAN'T SWIM BACK THROUGH THESE INFESTED WATERS!
AND I SEE NOTHING TO BUILD ANOTHER RAFT FROM!
SNAP!
LET'S SEARCH THE CITY! MAYBE THERE'S ANOTHER WAY OUT...
MEANWHILE, BACK ACROSS THE MARSH, THE INDIANS HAVE ARRIVED—
HEY! IT'S THE CRAZY MOUNTS OF THOSE THREE TROUBLEMAKERS! THEY'RE SEARCHING FOR MY FATHER'S SECRET CITY, TOO, EH?
!
!
Z
THEY MUST HAVE CROSSED THIS MARSH! MY FATHER USED TO TELL OF A "SWAMP OF DEATH" PROTECTING HIS "MINES OF FEAR"! LOOKS LIKE I'M ON THE VERGE OF GETTING AS RICH AS I'VE DREAMED!
BUT MAYBE I DON'T NEED TO LET MY BACKWARDS BROTHERS IN ON THE DEAL! THE LEGEND IS THAT OUR TRIBE IS SUPPOSED TO PROTECT THE CRYSTAL CITY, NOT LOOT IT! BAH!
MAKE ME A REED CANOE AND DO IT FAST! I GO ON ALONE FROM HERE!

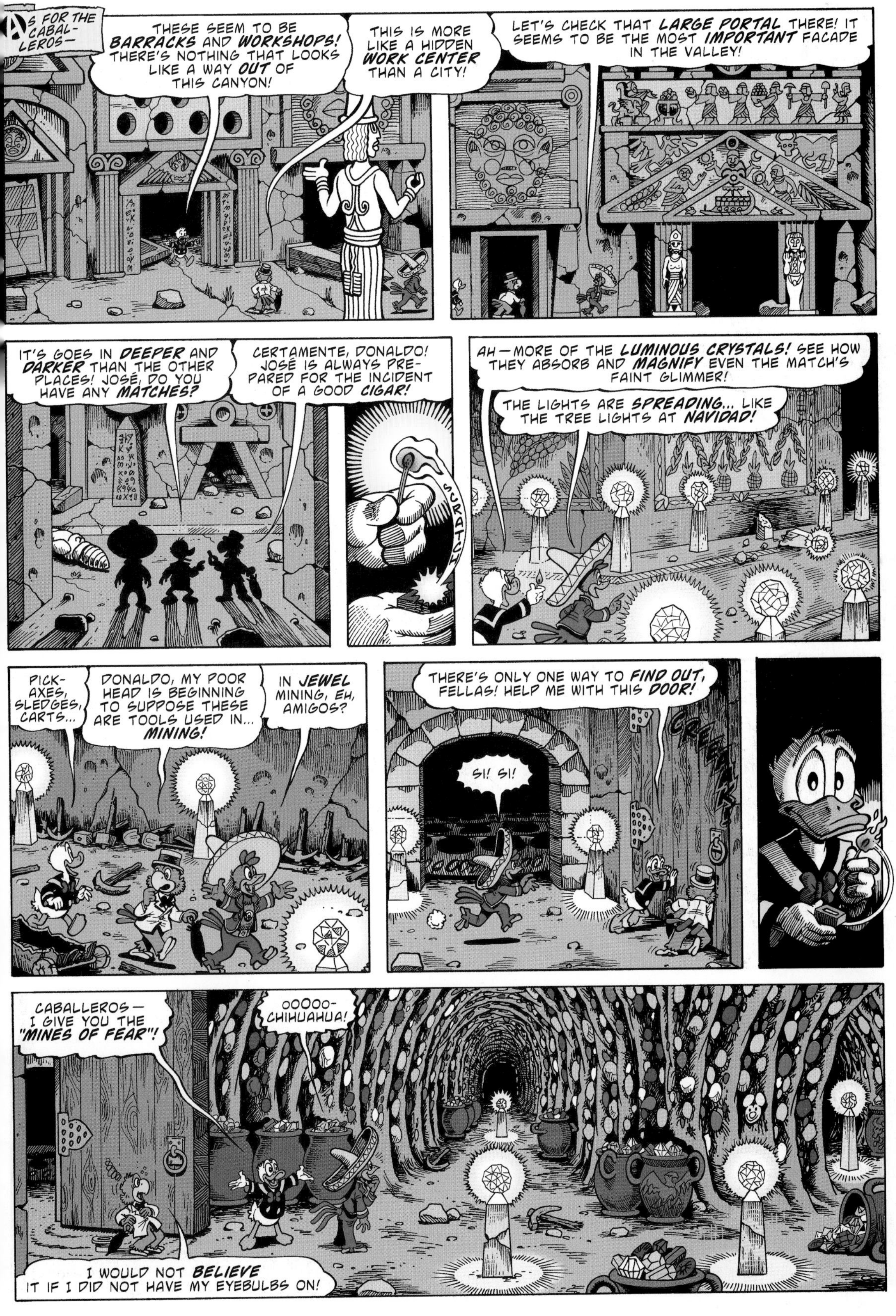
As for the caballeros—
THESE SEEM TO BE BARRACKS AND WORKSHOPS! THERE'S NOTHING THAT LOOKS LIKE A WAY OUT OF THIS CANYON!
THIS IS MORE LIKE A HIDDEN WORK CENTER THAN A CITY!
LET'S CHECK THAT LARGE PORTAL THERE! IT SEEMS TO BE THE MOST IMPORTANT FACADE IN THE VALLEY!
IT'S GOES IN DEEPER AND DARKER THAN THE OTHER PLACES! JOSÉ, DO YOU HAVE ANY MATCHES?
CERTAMENTE, DONALDO! JOSÉ IS ALWAYS PREPARED FOR THE INCIDENT OF A GOOD CIGAR!
SCRATCH
AH—MORE OF THE LUMINOUS CRYSTALS! SEE HOW THEY ABSORB AND MAGNIFY EVEN THE MATCH'S FAINT GLIMMER!
THE LIGHTS ARE SPREADING... LIKE THE TREE LIGHTS AT NAVIDAD!
PICK-AXES, SLEDGES, CARTS...
DONALDO, MY POOR HEAD IS BEGINNING TO SUPPOSE THESE ARE TOOLS USED IN... MINING!
IN JEWEL MINING, EH, AMIGOS?
THERE'S ONLY ONE WAY TO FIND OUT, FELLAS! HELP ME WITH THIS DOOR!
SI! SI!
CREEEAKK
CABALLEROS— I GIVE YOU THE "MINES OF FEAR"!
OOOOO-CHIHUAHUA!
I WOULD NOT BELIEVE IT IF I DID NOT HAVE MY EYEBULBS ON!

THIS MUST BE *MUITO* MINES ALL TOGETHER! DIAMONDS, EMERALDS, TOPAZES, AMETHYSTS, AQUAMARINES...

YOU SURE KNOW YOUR *GEMSTONES*, JOSÉ!

AH, I KNOW HOW THE *SENHORITAS* LIKE THE *GIFTS* OF THE PRETTY BAUBLES, AMIGO!

THIS MINE WOULD KEEP *EVERY GATINHA* IN RIO HAPPY!

AND IN CHIHUAHUA!

BUT COULD THIS MINE *REALLY* HAVE BEEN DUG BY EUROPEANS WHO WERE HERE *BEFORE* THE PORTUGESE CAME IN 1500?

DONAL', WHAT DOES YOUR JUNIOR GOPHER BOOKLET ABOUT BRAZIL SAY?

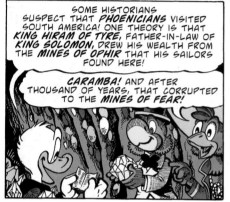

SOME HISTORIANS SUSPECT THAT *PHOENICIANS* VISITED SOUTH AMERICA! ONE THEORY IS THAT *KING HIRAM OF TYRE*, FATHER-IN-LAW OF *KING SOLOMON*, DREW HIS WEALTH FROM THE *MINES OF OPHIR* THAT HIS SAILORS FOUND HERE!

CARAMBA! AND AFTER THOUSAND OF YEARS, THAT CORRUPTED TO THE *MINES OF FEAR!*

OBA! PERHAPS WE HAVE FOUND *KING SOLOMON'S MINES* THEM-SELVES!

NO, THOSE ARE IN *ARABIA!*

DON'T TELL ME— YOU KNOW THAT BECAUSE *YOU FOUND* KING SOLOMON'S MINES?

WITH YOUR OLD ONCLE SCRUNCH HELPING YOU, DONAL'?

WELL... YEAH... I GUESS SO...

WHAT A *HERO!* ADVENTURE AND TREASURE FALLS OFF TREES LIKE *RIPE AVOCADOS* WHEN DONAL' WALKS BY!

AND HE SAID HE FELT *UNIMPORTANT* AND *DULL!* DONALDO JUST DIDN'T WANT *US* TO FEEL SO BAD ABOUT *OUR* LIVES! WHAT A *FINE AMIGO!*

WE MAY HAVE FOUND THE MINES OF OPHIR, BUT WE'RE STILL *TRAPPED* HERE! I NEED TO *THINK*...

OH! WATCH OUT FOR THAT *SNAKE*, YOU GUYS! ALTHOUGH HE LOOKS *HARMLESS!*

!

WE KNOW YOU ARE A *MACHO HOMBRE*, DONAL', BUT ARE YOU *CERTAIN* THAT SNAKE IS *HARMLESS?*

WELL, I'LL *LOOK IT UP* IN THE WOODCHUCK PAMPHLET IF YOU *INSIST!*

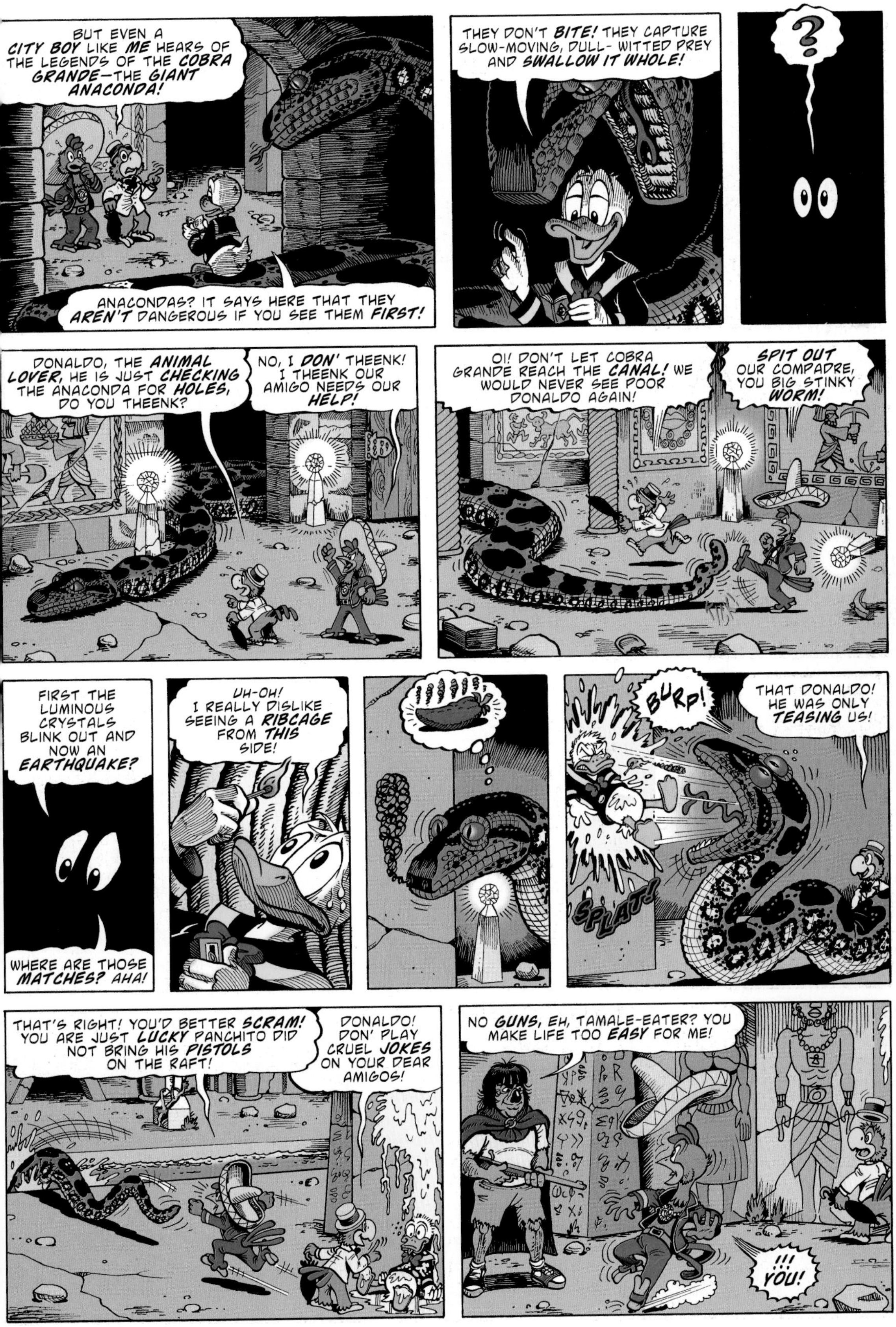
BUT EVEN A CITY BOY LIKE ME HEARS OF THE LEGENDS OF THE COBRA GRANDE—THE GIANT ANACONDA!
ANACONDAS? IT SAYS HERE THAT THEY AREN'T DANGEROUS IF YOU SEE THEM FIRST!
THEY DON'T BITE! THEY CAPTURE SLOW-MOVING, DULL-WITTED PREY AND SWALLOW IT WHOLE!
?
DONALDO, THE ANIMAL LOVER, HE IS JUST CHECKING THE ANACONDA FOR HOLES, DO YOU THEENK?
NO, I DON' THEENK! I THEENK OUR AMIGO NEEDS OUR HELP!
OI! DON'T LET COBRA GRANDE REACH THE CANAL! WE WOULD NEVER SEE POOR DONALDO AGAIN!
SPIT OUT OUR COMPADRE, YOU BIG STINKY WORM!
FIRST THE LUMINOUS CRYSTALS BLINK OUT AND NOW AN EARTHQUAKE?
WHERE ARE THOSE MATCHES? AHA!
UH-OH! I REALLY DISLIKE SEEING A RIBCAGE FROM THIS SIDE!
BURP!
THAT DONALDO! HE WAS ONLY TEASING US!
SPLAT!
THAT'S RIGHT! YOU'D BETTER SCRAM! YOU ARE JUST LUCKY PANCHITO DID NOT BRING HIS PISTOLS ON THE RAFT!
DONALDO! DON' PLAY CRUEL JOKES ON YOUR DEAR AMIGOS!
NO GUNS, EH, TAMALE-EATER? YOU MAKE LIFE TOO EASY FOR ME!
!!! YOU!

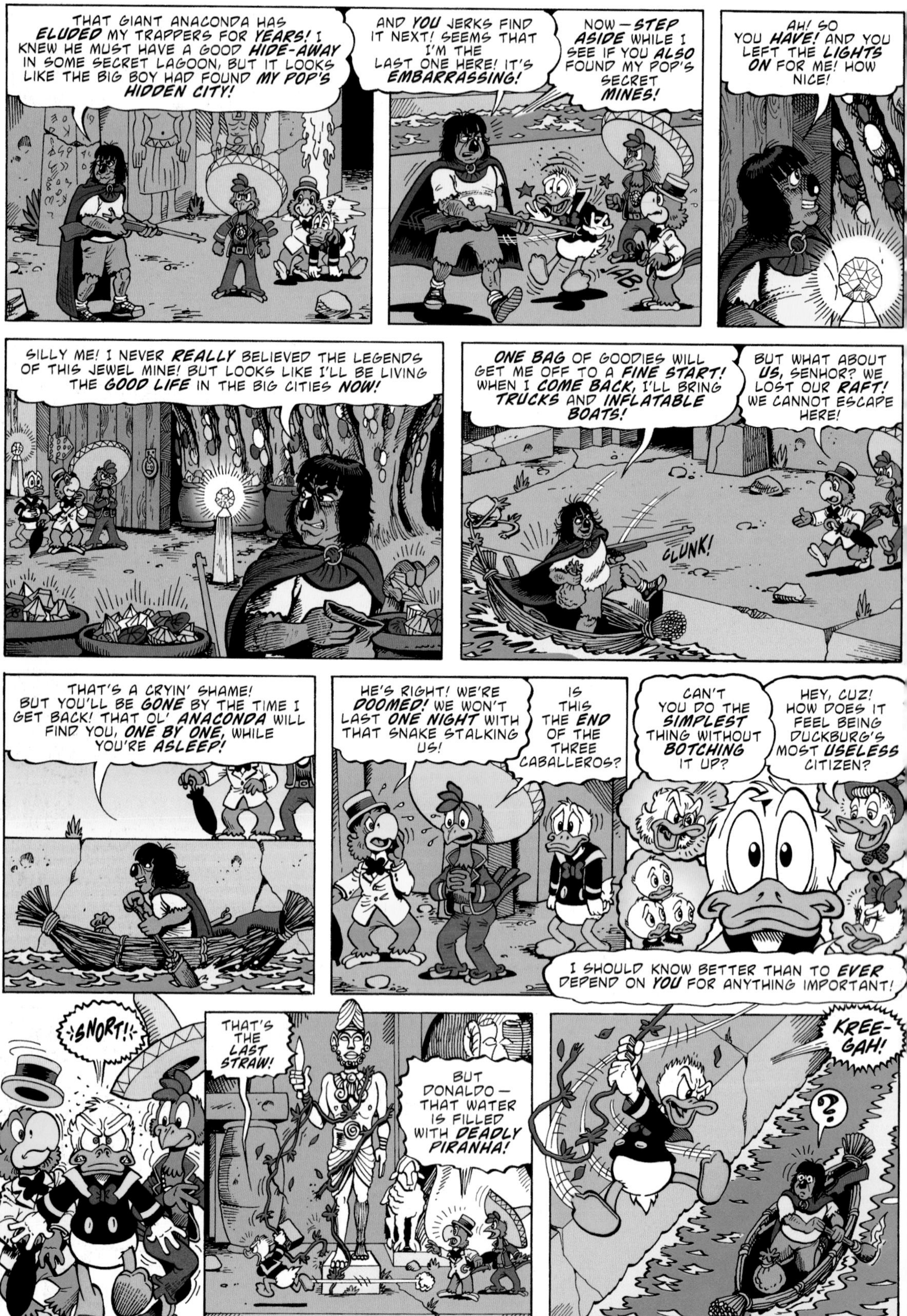
THAT GIANT ANACONDA HAS ELUDED MY TRAPPERS FOR YEARS! I KNEW HE MUST HAVE A GOOD HIDE-AWAY IN SOME SECRET LAGOON, BUT IT LOOKS LIKE THE BIG BOY HAD FOUND MY POP'S HIDDEN CITY!
AND YOU JERKS FIND IT NEXT! SEEMS THAT I'M THE LAST ONE HERE! IT'S EMBARRASSING!
NOW—STEP ASIDE WHILE I SEE IF YOU ALSO FOUND MY POP'S SECRET MINES!
AH! SO YOU HAVE! AND YOU LEFT THE LIGHTS ON FOR ME! HOW NICE!
SILLY ME! I NEVER REALLY BELIEVED THE LEGENDS OF THIS JEWEL MINE! BUT LOOKS LIKE I'LL BE LIVING THE GOOD LIFE IN THE BIG CITIES NOW!
ONE BAG OF GOODIES WILL GET ME OFF TO A FINE START! WHEN I COME BACK, I'LL BRING TRUCKS AND INFLATABLE BOATS!
BUT WHAT ABOUT US, SENHOR? WE LOST OUR RAFT! WE CANNOT ESCAPE HERE!
CLUNK!
THAT'S A CRYIN' SHAME! BUT YOU'LL BE GONE BY THE TIME I GET BACK! THAT OL' ANACONDA WILL FIND YOU, ONE BY ONE, WHILE YOU'RE ASLEEP!
HE'S RIGHT! WE'RE DOOMED! WE WON'T LAST ONE NIGHT WITH THAT SNAKE STALKING US!
IS THIS THE END OF THE THREE CABALLEROS?
CAN'T YOU DO THE SIMPLEST THING WITHOUT BOTCHING IT UP?
HEY, CUZ! HOW DOES IT FEEL BEING DUCKBURG'S MOST USELESS CITIZEN?
I SHOULD KNOW BETTER THAN TO EVER DEPEND ON YOU FOR ANYTHING IMPORTANT!
SNORT!
THAT'S THE LAST STRAW!
BUT DONALDO—THAT WATER IS FILLED WITH DEADLY PIRANHA!
KREE-GAH!
?

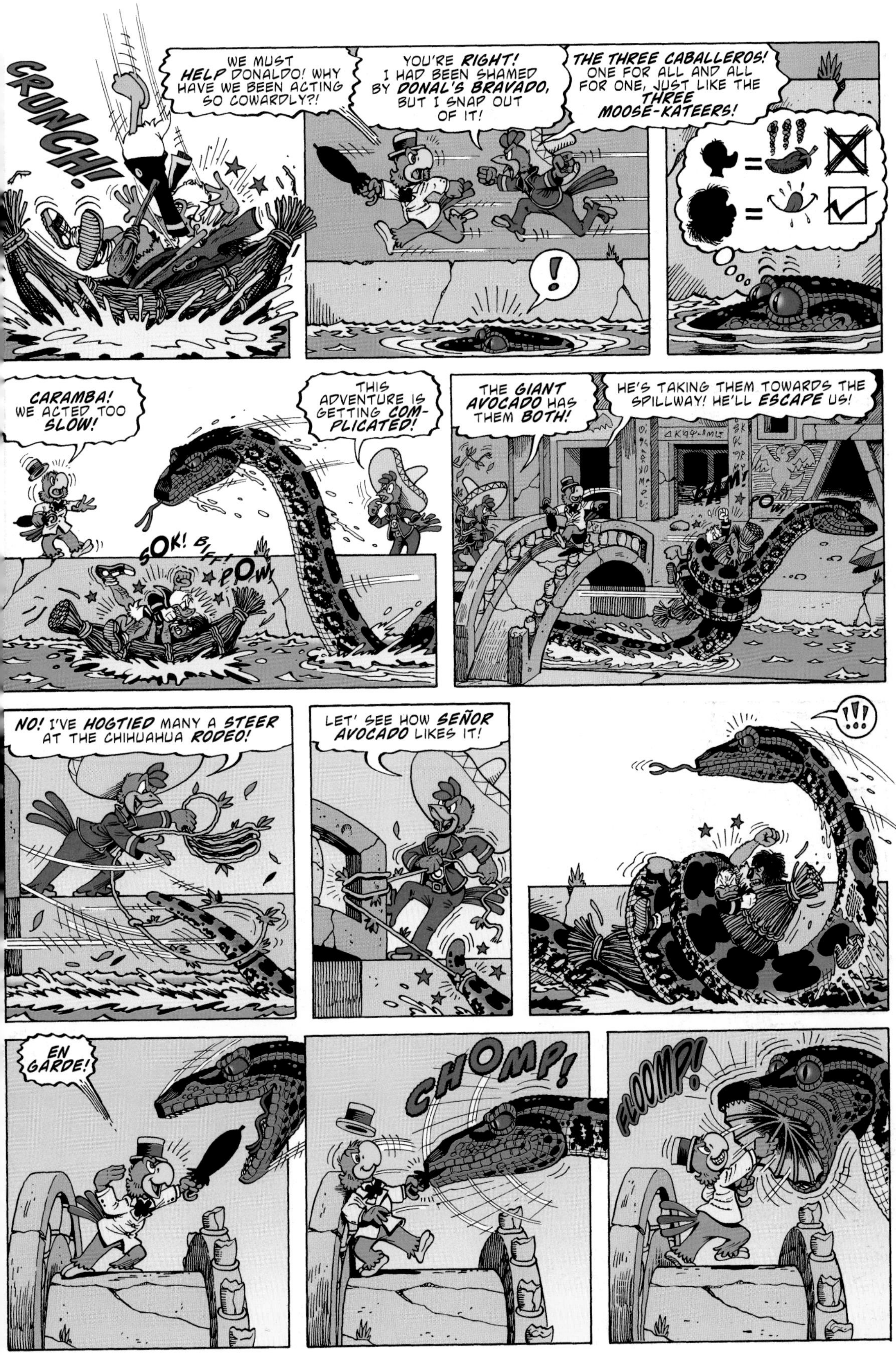
CRUNCH!
WE MUST HELP DONALDO! WHY HAVE WE BEEN ACTING SO COWARDLY?!
YOU'RE RIGHT! I HAD BEEN SHAMED BY DONAL'S BRAVADO, BUT I SNAP OUT OF IT!
THE THREE CABALLEROS! ONE FOR ALL AND ALL FOR ONE, JUST LIKE THE THREE MOOSE-KATEERS!
!
CARAMBA! WE ACTED TOO SLOW!
THIS ADVENTURE IS GETTING COM-PLICATED!
SOK! BIFF! POW!
THE GIANT AVOCADO HAS THEM BOTH!
HE'S TAKING THEM TOWARDS THE SPILLWAY! HE'LL ESCAPE US!
POW
NO! I'VE HOGTIED MANY A STEER AT THE CHIHUAHUA RODEO!
LET' SEE HOW SEÑOR AVOCADO LIKES IT!
!!!
EN GARDE!
CHOMP!
FLOOMP!

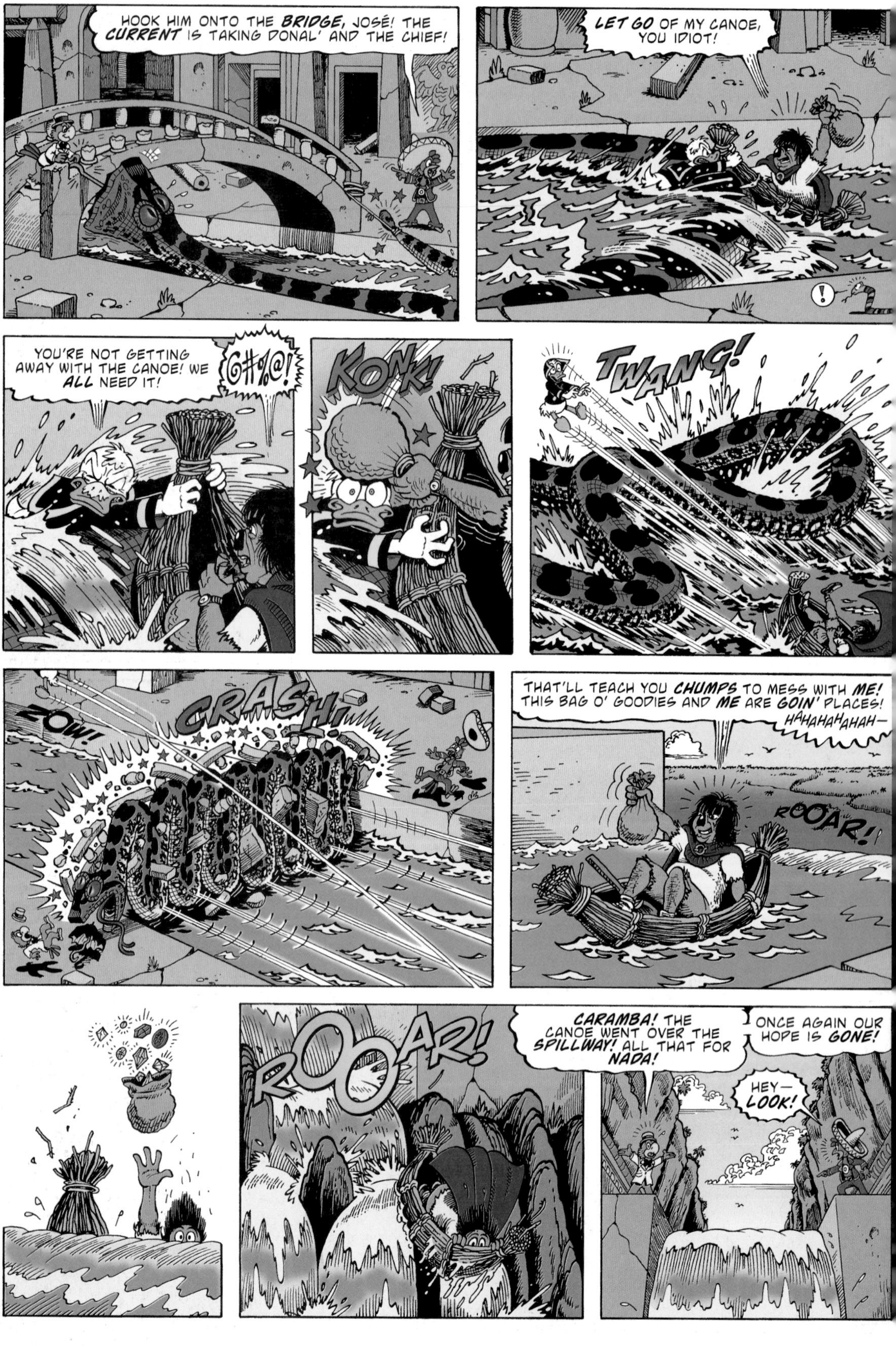
HOOK HIM ONTO THE BRIDGE, JOSÉ! THE CURRENT IS TAKING DONAL' AND THE CHIEF!
LET GO OF MY CANOE, YOU IDIOT!
!
YOU'RE NOT GETTING AWAY WITH THE CANOE! WE ALL NEED IT!
@#%@!
KONK!
TWANG!
ZOW!
CRASH!
THAT'LL TEACH YOU CHUMPS TO MESS WITH ME! THIS BAG O' GOODIES AND ME ARE GOIN' PLACES! HAHAHAHAHAH—
ROOAR!
ROOAR!
CARAMBA! THE CANOE WENT OVER THE SPILLWAY! ALL THAT FOR NADA!
ONCE AGAIN OUR HOPE IS GONE!
HEY— LOOK!

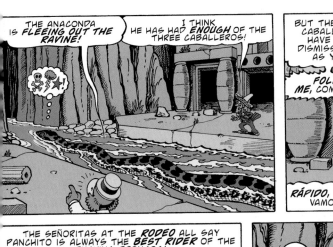

THE ANACONDA IS *FLEEING OUT THE RAVINE!*

I THINK HE HAS HAD *ENOUGH* OF THE THREE CABALLEROS!

BUT THE THREE CABALLEROS HAVE *NOT* DISMISSED HIM AS YET!

FOLLOW ME, COMPADRES!

RÁPIDO, DONALDO! *VAMOS LÁ!*

THE SEÑORITAS AT THE *RODEO* ALL SAY PANCHITO IS ALWAYS THE *BEST RIDER* OF THE BUCKING BRONCOS!

?

GUK!

HOLD ON, CABALLEROS!

WE ARE *LEAVING* THE CRYSTAL CITY IN *HIGH STYLE!*

WAIT UNTIL SEÑOR MARTINEZ SEES *THIS!*

YEE-HAW!

RIDE 'EM, VAQUERO!

BROTHER, *THAT'S* ACTION!

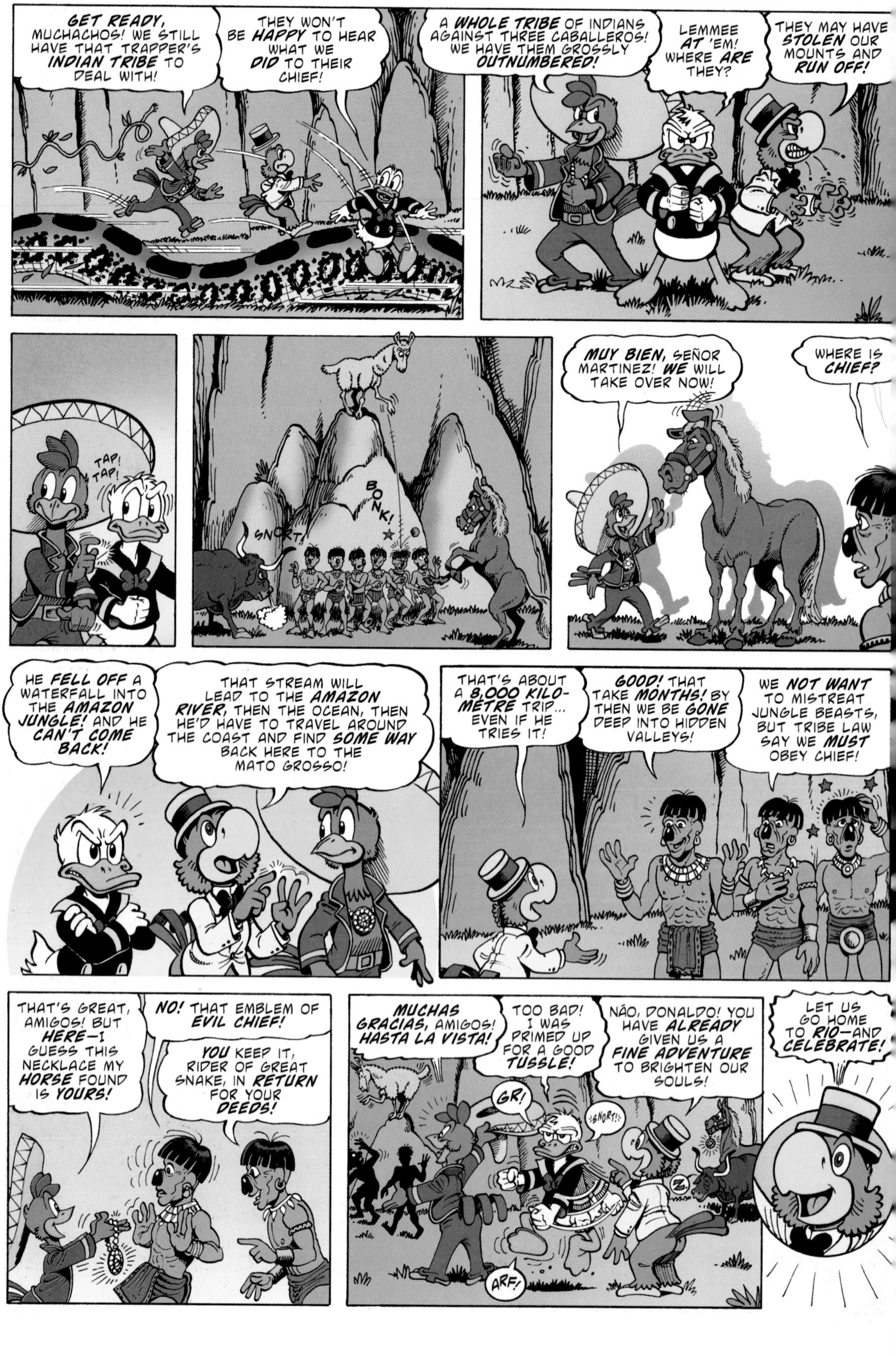

GET READY, MUCHACHOS! WE STILL HAVE THAT TRAPPER'S INDIAN TRIBE TO DEAL WITH!
THEY WON'T BE HAPPY TO HEAR WHAT WE DID TO THEIR CHIEF!
A WHOLE TRIBE OF INDIANS AGAINST THREE CABALLEROS! WE HAVE THEM GROSSLY OUTNUMBERED!
LEMMEE AT 'EM! WHERE ARE THEY?
THEY MAY HAVE STOLEN OUR MOUNTS AND RUN OFF!
TAP! TAP!
SNORT!
BONK!
MUY BIEN, SEÑOR MARTINEZ! WE WILL TAKE OVER NOW!
WHERE IS CHIEF?
HE FELL OFF A WATERFALL INTO THE AMAZON JUNGLE! AND HE CAN'T COME BACK!
THAT STREAM WILL LEAD TO THE AMAZON RIVER, THEN THE OCEAN, THEN HE'D HAVE TO TRAVEL AROUND THE COAST AND FIND SOME WAY BACK HERE TO THE MATO GROSSO!
THAT'S ABOUT A 8,000 KILO-METRE TRIP... EVEN IF HE TRIES IT!
GOOD! THAT TAKE MONTHS! BY THEN WE BE GONE DEEP INTO HIDDEN VALLEYS!
WE NOT WANT TO MISTREAT JUNGLE BEASTS, BUT TRIBE LAW SAY WE MUST OBEY CHIEF!
THAT'S GREAT, AMIGOS! BUT HERE—I GUESS THIS NECKLACE MY HORSE FOUND IS YOURS!
NO! THAT EMBLEM OF EVIL CHIEF!
YOU KEEP IT, RIDER OF GREAT SNAKE, IN RETURN FOR YOUR DEEDS!
MUCHAS GRACIAS, AMIGOS! HASTA LA VISTA!
TOO BAD! I WAS PRIMED UP FOR A GOOD TUSSLE!
NÃO, DONALDO! YOU HAVE ALREADY GIVEN US A FINE ADVENTURE TO BRIGHTEN OUR SOULS!
LET US GO HOME TO RIO—AND CELEBRATE!
GR!
SNORT!
Z
ARF!

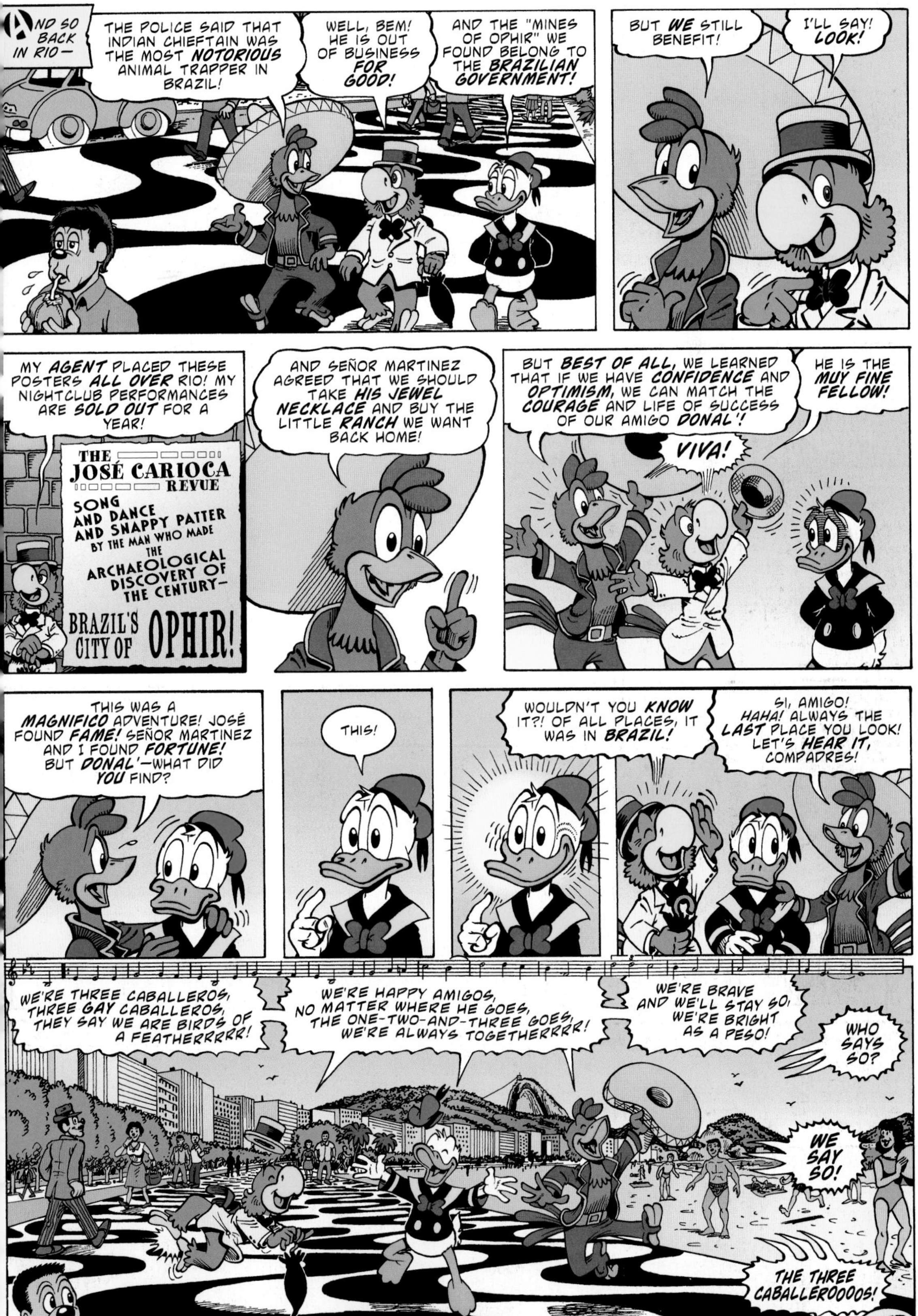
AND SO BACK IN RIO—
THE POLICE SAID THAT INDIAN CHIEFTAIN WAS THE MOST NOTORIOUS ANIMAL TRAPPER IN BRAZIL!
WELL, BEM! HE IS OUT OF BUSINESS FOR GOOD!
AND THE "MINES OF OPHIR" WE FOUND BELONG TO THE BRAZILIAN GOVERNMENT!
BUT WE STILL BENEFIT!
I'LL SAY! LOOK!
MY AGENT PLACED THESE POSTERS ALL OVER RIO! MY NIGHTCLUB PERFORMANCES ARE SOLD OUT FOR A YEAR!
THE JOSÉ CARIOCA REVUE
SONG AND DANCE AND SNAPPY PATTER BY THE MAN WHO MADE THE ARCHAEOLOGICAL DISCOVERY OF THE CENTURY—
BRAZIL'S CITY OF OPHIR!
AND SEÑOR MARTINEZ AGREED THAT WE SHOULD TAKE HIS JEWEL NECKLACE AND BUY THE LITTLE RANCH WE WANT BACK HOME!
BUT BEST OF ALL, WE LEARNED THAT IF WE HAVE CONFIDENCE AND OPTIMISM, WE CAN MATCH THE COURAGE AND LIFE OF SUCCESS OF OUR AMIGO DONAL'!
HE IS THE MUY FINE FELLOW!
VIVA!
THIS WAS A MAGNIFICO ADVENTURE! JOSÉ FOUND FAME! SEÑOR MARTINEZ AND I FOUND FORTUNE! BUT DONAL'—WHAT DID YOU FIND?
THIS!
WOULDN'T YOU KNOW IT?! OF ALL PLACES, IT WAS IN BRAZIL!
SI, AMIGO! HAHA! ALWAYS THE LAST PLACE YOU LOOK! LET'S HEAR IT, COMPADRES!
WE'RE THREE CABALLEROS, THREE GAY CABALLEROS, THEY SAY WE ARE BIRDS OF A FEATHERRRRR!
WE'RE HAPPY AMIGOS, NO MATTER WHERE HE GOES, THE ONE-TWO-AND-THREE GOES, WE'RE ALWAYS TOGETHERRRR!
WE'RE BRAVE AND WE'LL STAY SO, WE'RE BRIGHT AS A PESO!
WHO SAYS SO?
WE SAY SO!
THE THREE CABALLEROOOOS!
END

SHIVER ME FROZEN TAILFEATHERS!

TWO FROSTY TALES FROM THE SNOWY BADLANDS OF THE YUKON!

GEMSTONE PUBLISHING

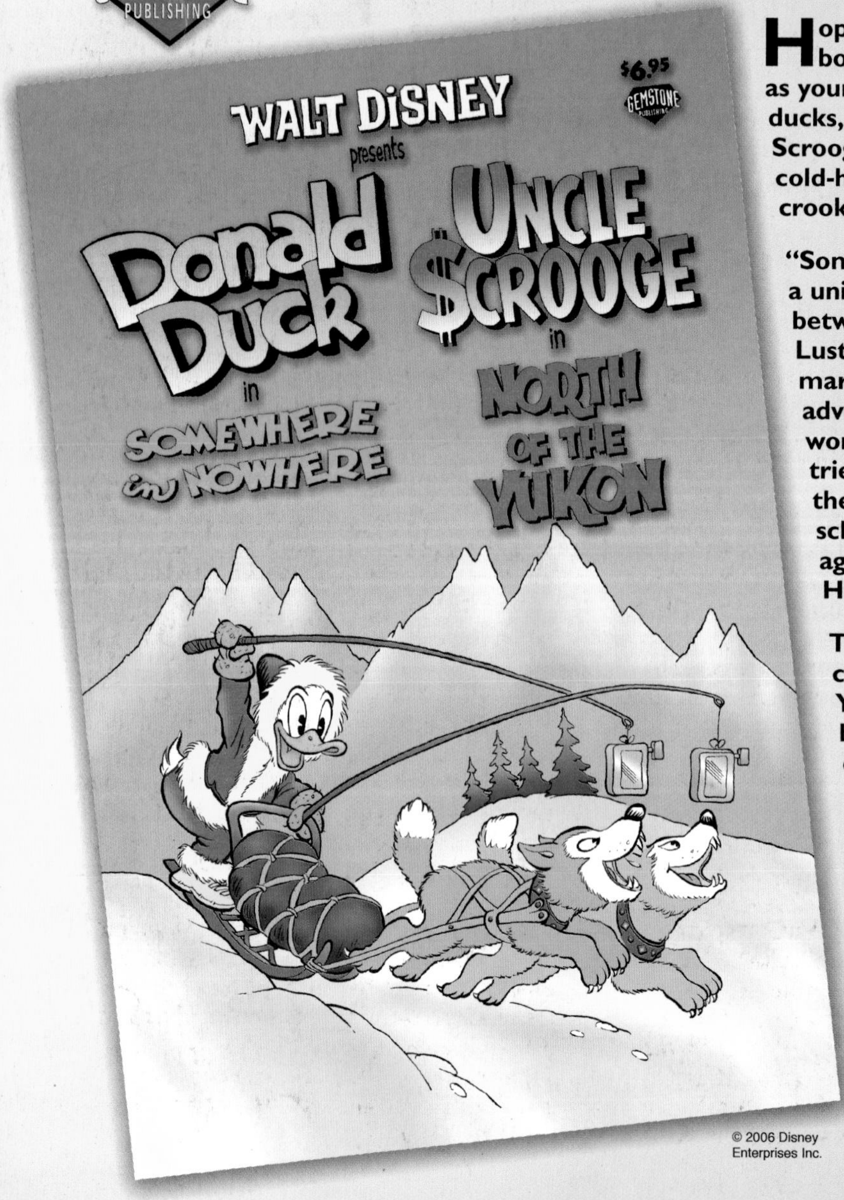
$6.95
WALT DISNEY
presents
GEMSTONE PUBLISHING
Donald Duck
in
SOMEWHERE in NOWHERE
UNCLE $CROOGE
in
NORTH OF THE YUKON

Hop aboard a dogsled bound for adventure as your favorite Disney ducks, Donald and Uncle Scrooge, tangle with some cold-hearted Klondike crooks!

"Somewhere in Nowhere," a unique collaboration between Carl Barks, John Lustig, and Pat Block, marks the last duck adventure on which Barks worked! When Donald tries to get rich in Alaska, the money-making scheme leads to a race against time with the evil Hamalot McSwine!

Then, in Barks' 1965 classic "North of the Yukon," the race is between Scrooge and old-time rival Soapy Slick… with the stakes involving an IOU that could impound the McDuck millions!

***Donald Duck and Uncle Scrooge*—two feature-length duck epics in one $6.95, 64-page trade paperback. Mush, you huskies!**